CRASH INTO YOU

CRASH INTO YOU

Diana Morland

Crash Into You © Diana Morland.
Paperback Edition.
Edited by Elizabeth Peters.
Cover design by Kit Tunstall.

First LoveLight Press print publication: December 2016.
http://lovelightpress.com

Crash Into You is set in Philadelphia, USA, and as such uses American English throughout.

CONTENTS

CHAPTER 1

Megan was nearly to the pack, just ahead. She stretched to reach them, her skates whizzing along. She could see the crowd speeding by out of the corner of her eye, she could hear them screaming in excitement, but she couldn't focus on them. All she could see were the blockers just ahead of her. She'd already made lead jammer; now was the time to start racking up the points.

The girl at the back of the pack was all in blue and black—on Megan's team, Monstrous Regiment. She couldn't see details as she sped past, but she could see the other woman moving up to join her, to clear her way through the other team, Rolling in the Street. They were a new team to her; Monstrous Regiment was playing them for the very first time, now that they'd gotten their WFTDA membership.

Megan intended to show them that just because they were all members now didn't mean that they couldn't be pounded right into the floor.

She whizzed right past the first woman in red and vaguely heard the crowd noise increase as the announcer shouted, "And the first point goes to Monstrous Regiment, Margaret Splatwood making her way past Britney Scares with no hesitation!"

But the next blocker was more difficult. She flung her arm out to stop Megan, slowing her down long enough to read her name—Kiss With a Fist.

That didn't stop Megan. She had too much momentum and too much adrenaline. It had been another long, nerve-wracking week at work, and Megan wasn't going to let *anything* stop her from winning this match for her team.

Careful not to use her elbows (she did not want to get a penalty during the first jam), she wrangled her way past Kiss With a Fist, spinning on her skates to get past her—but pass her she did.

The crowd cheered again, the announcer booming barely louder than they were even with amplification. "Another point to Monstrous Regiment! But Jane Bowie Knife is catching up to the pack there—it won't take much for Rolling in the Street to make this a tie."

That strengthened Megan's determination even more. She put on another powerful burst of speed with her skates. The next blocker's shirt said Mountain Bruise, and she was thick with curves. Megan was sure she could speed past her, on her left, before she could react.

But Mountain Bruise was too quick for her. The shorter woman glanced over her shoulder with a red-lipped smirk, then turned sideways, kicking her skate to get just a little backward momentum. Megan collided directly with a lush, well-padded, red-spandex-covered ass.

The world seemed to slow down as she bounced off Mountain Bruise's backside, her skates skidding slightly as their momentum was reversed. Her thighs felt warm where the blocker had collided with her. That grin was back on Mountain Bruise's face, and it was the last thing Megan saw before her skates slid out from under her and she went down onto the floor.

Time returned to its normal speed and the pack shot past her. Jane Bowie Knife had caught up with the pack now and was wrestling with Mary Shelley's Monster. She was going to erase Megan's lead in a moment.

It wasn't a bad fall; she'd only had the breath knocked out of her for a second. She jumped back to her feet and took off on her skates again, getting back in bounds and catching up to the pack in no time at all. Jane Bowie Knife had made it past the first blocker, but this time Sir Blocksalot slammed her way through the pack, getting ahead of Jane Bowie Knife and clearing a path for Megan.

Sir Blocksalot hip-checked Mountain Bruise aside as Megan caught up to them. It was hard to argue with Sir

Blocksalot's broad frame packed with muscle; Megan grinned at Mountain Bruise as she whipped past. That was three more Rolling in the Street players she'd passed, and she wasn't going to let a little fall get in her way.

Mountain Bruise just grinned back.

The girls ran at each other and collapsed in the middle of the locker room, a huge, hugging, screaming, pile. "Three, two, one," called Shelly, the team captain, and together they all screamed, "MONSTERS!"

"Great job out there, ladies!" Shelly screamed. "Let 'em know that the Monstrous Regiment are the *rulers of them all!* Now let's get shitfaced and recover!"

Megan screamed along with all the rest of them. She was covered in sweat, she had at least three new bruises forming, and she couldn't be happier.

The Monstrous Regiment had just thoroughly beaten Rolling in the Streets, 209 to 76. Megan hadn't skated in every jam, but she'd been jammer in almost a third—nearly a hundred of those points were hers. And she hadn't let Mountain Bruise knock her down again. They just seemed to brush past each other... a lot.

She could still feel warmth where Mountain Bruise's hand had brushed against her lower back in the last jam. Probably just sweat. She needed to change.

Megan spat out her mouth guard, then pulled off her helmet, followed by her gloves, and tossed them into her bag. Kristine—or Patty Whack, another of the team's jammers—clapped her on the shoulder. "Really nice work out there, Splatwood."

Megan grinned and clapped Kristine's shoulder in return. "Not too bad yourself, Patty. I loved the way you got low to get under Kiss with a Fist's arm."

Kristine snorted. "Yeah, right. I didn't do anything special—I'm just short. The way you matched Gayle's skates perfectly so the pack couldn't stop you from getting through in the first jam—now that was impressive."

Megan laughed, but she appreciated the compliment. Roller derby was everything to her, and she had been working extra hard the last few months. It was nice to not only feel the practice paying off, but know that other people could see it, too.

They chatted while they stripped out of their derby uniforms. Shelly came by halfway through to pat them on the backs. "Good work, both of you. Anybody injured? All your joints all working correctly?"

"All good here," Megan reported, flexing her fingers, toes, elbows, and knees. She was bruised in plenty of places, but none of those bruises were likely to interfere with her movement. Dealing with bruises she could do—she was very familiar with bruises.

"Your ass okay after that fall early on?" Shelly asked.

"It's fine, but if you want to kiss it and make sure, that's okay with me," Megan said, smirking and grabbing her T-shirt from the locker she was using.

Shelly laid a kiss on her forehead instead. "You want a ride to the bar? We're meeting Rolling in the Streets there."

"Sounds good," Megan said, not willing to pass up the offer of a ride but suddenly nervous. They'd gone drinking with the opposing teams in the past, so what was bothering her now? It might just be that Rolling in the Streets had been beaten so thoroughly. She knew she shouldn't gloat, but it might be hard to avoid it.

As she put her normal clothes back on, her mind wandered back, again, to the embarrassing way she'd bounced off Mountain Bruise's ass in the first jam. That padding must be a real asset—no pun intended—to her team. Mountain Bruise probably hadn't even felt it, and Megan had gone head-over-heels, her gangly arms and legs unable to catch enough air to slow her fall.

Megan shook her head at herself. She might be tall, but she was fast and she could slip through gaps. She was one of the reasons her team had beaten the opposition so hard today, and she wasn't going to let a set of lush curves distract her from that.

CHAPTER 2

As soon as Megan walked into the bar behind Shelly, someone shoved a beer bottle into her hand. She lifted it in the air to toast her benefactor—Lisa, also known as Jenny Greenteeth and the oldest member of the team—and then pulled it to her mouth to guzzle half the bottle. She was too anxious and tense, even after pouring out all her adrenaline into the game. The alcohol would help her loosen up.

With that in her system, she moved further into the room. It was crowded, but most of the people there were derby girls. Megan either knew them from the team or recognized them from tonight's game. Of course, her eyes picked out Mountain Bruise immediately. The curvy blocker was bent over, legging-covered ass provocatively in the air as she talked to... a little kid, actually.

Was there really a kid in the bar? She was wearing a

pink ballerina outfit, complete with tulle tutu, and she looked perfectly happy to be talking to Mountain Bruise. It was pretty adorable, actually. Megan felt her heart flutter a little bit. She rolled her eyes at herself and took another swig of her beer.

When she lowered her head again, there was another woman bending over the little girl and lifting her up in her arms. Megan was pretty sure she was another player on Rolling in the Streets—something like Kate? One of them was probably the kid's mom, then.

She turned away to scan the rest of the room. There were plenty of other interesting people here to talk to. She found Kristine, Tara, and Gayle talking in a small knot and went to join them.

"Hey there, Blocksalot," she said, slinging an arm around Gayle's broad shoulders. "My heroine."

Gayle laughed and pushed Megan's arm off her shoulders. "Get off me, tall and skinny."

Megan pretended to pout. Tara laughed at her and said, "I watched you guys. That was pretty impressive. Had you ever rehearsed following each other like that?"

"Rehearsed it?" Gayle said. "I didn't even know she was behind me until we'd passed two blockers. I was just trying to get to the front of the pack to be an impenetrable wall in case Jane Bowie Knife made it through."

"My name is Ruth," said Jane Bowie Knife, joining their circle with a fruity-looking drink in her hand. "Nice to meet all of you. That was a really good game."

The four members of Monstrous Regiment introduced themselves, shook Ruth's hand, and complimented her, but Megan knew they were just being polite. Ruth had gotten a few points for her team, but it was hard to be generous about another team's performance after the way they'd just flattened them.

In fact, after a few more exchanges, Megan lost interest in the conversation and walked away to look for another beer. She didn't want to hang around and make nice with the other team. She wanted to revel in victory and spend half the day tomorrow sleeping it off before she had to go back to work on Monday.

When she had her new beer in her hand and turned away from the bar, she found herself face-to-face with Mountain Bruise. Her breath hitched and she took an involuntary half-step back. The other woman was short, but she had an enormous presence that had little to do with the size of her ass—or her tits, which, as Megan could now see, were equally magnificent, shown off to great effect in a black V-neck shirt.

"Hi," Mountain Bruise said, her mouth curving in a wicked grin. She'd removed her bright makeup, but the smile was still the same one she'd worn on the track. "I figured I could introduce myself to you now that we're not fighting against each other. You're damn good."

Megan grinned at her, trying—but sure she was failing—to put the same degree of confidence and insouciance in her own smile. "Yeah, you, too. Or at least your ass is."

Dammit, why couldn't she be confident and competent at anything other than roller derby? She'd worked so hard at it, and she knew she was good, and it had made a huge difference in her life—but she still stumbled over her tongue when she spoke, and she still couldn't find anything her life she was good at except for roller derby.

Oh well, maybe that didn't matter. All she needed was derby. Work 40 hours a week, derby 20, that was a good balance. As long as those paychecks kept her in derby gear and booze.

Mountain Bruise laughed loudly, flinging her hand into the air—the hand that wasn't holding her red wine. "Oh, that's a good one! Yeah," she continued, slapping her own ass so that it jiggled, "those hours I've put in training with wine and lasagna have really paid off."

Megan had meant it as more of an insult, but she laughed along anyway and swigged her beer. Even her insults didn't come out right. Could Mountain Bruise tell that Megan was seriously attracted to her? It felt wrong to be so into the opposition. She had to get away.

With her head tilted back, she darted her gaze around the room. Who could she go talk to as an excuse to escape from her rival?

There was Helen—she'd played pivot to Megan's blocker a few times tonight, and once Megan had ended up having to pass her the star, giving up the lead jammer position to her teammate. She could use the excuse of wanting to talk tactics with her. The passing hadn't gone as smoothly as it could have; it would be useful to talk to Helen anyway.

"Mountain Bruise—" she started.

"It's Gianna," the other player said, holding her hand out confidently. "And I'm guessing your name isn't really Margaret. Though I could be wrong about that—our pirate girls use their real first names."

"Uh, no, it's Megan," Megan said, reaching out awkwardly to shake Gianna's hand. The other woman's fingers were just as plump as the rest of her, and her grip was firm and aggressive. Megan felt herself just a little more attracted, even if she was also confused. "I just really like Margaret Atwood."

"Me, too," Gianna said, her eyes lighting up. "*The Handmaid's Tale* was practically life-changing."

"Literally life-changing," Megan said, her heart seeming to twist a little. Her rival loved Margaret Atwood too?

Gianna nodded hard. "It really puts a mirror on society. Once I'd read it, I knew what people were talking about when they complained about the patriarchy."

"Exactly." Megan grinned back at her for a moment before remembering they were rivals. She had to get away and talk to Helen—but first she needed to understand what Gianna had been talking about a minute ago. "Who are the pirate girls?"

"Mary Read and Grace O'Malley," Gianna said, turning—she swiveled her whole body from the hips—to point at two girls who looked to be older teens, both of them with pale red hair and freckles. "They're sisters, and their names really are Mary and Grace."

Megan nodded. She remembered seeing those two on the track. "They work well together."

"They ought to, they grew up that way. We're going to flatten you next time, you know."

Megan laughed. She was on familiar territory again. "You wish. We creamed the floor with you today. You couldn't practice enough to get ahead of us." She took a swig of her beer. It was empty already. She groped around for the bar to put it out of her way.

"Oh yeah?" Gianna looked Megan up and down until Megan felt tingles throughout her spine. "I think we can work as hard as you. Harder." Her smile changed—tightened. The smack talk was just beginning.

Megan crossed her arms. "I'll believe it when I see it. And we're ready to knock you down on the track as many times as it takes to convince you otherwise." Now she was in her element—these might be words, but the words were about roller derby. Adrenaline rushed through her. It wasn't quite the heady, addictive feeling she got from derby itself, but it sure felt good.

"I'm ready to get up just as many times as you knock me down, babe." Gianna winked. "When do you practice?"

"Every Tuesday night, Thursday night, and Saturday morning. More in the off-season, when we're not playing every weekend. Otherwise we'll get flabby and out of shape."

She raised her eyebrows. Maybe this time Gianna would take the insult as it was meant.

"Hmm." Gianna gulped down her wine, until her glass, too, was empty. She reached past Megan to place it on the bar, her arm—and then her breasts—brushing against Megan's elbow. Megan dropped her arms and stepped to the side, getting out of the way.

But Gianna turned to her again. "You look like you're in pretty good shape to me." Then she stepped forward, right into Megan's personal space, put one hand on the back of her neck, and pulled her head down to kiss her.

Surprised—and already turned on—Megan kissed her back, their lips hot and wet, tangy with their respective drinks. She could feel Gianna's incredible curves just barely brushing against her and longed to get closer to them.

But she shouldn't—she couldn't. Gianna was—

Wait. She was single, and she could kiss whoever she damn well pleased. Sometimes it was hard to remember that, even now.

And if she pleased to kiss Gianna, or maybe a little more than that, so what? Nobody on her team would care. If members of the other team cared, well, Megan didn't give a crap about them, other than how they played roller derby.

It didn't matter if she was into Gianna just because she was a good derby player and a strong opponent. This was a moment to seize, and she was seizing it.

She put her arms on Gianna's waist and turned them gently without disengaging their lips. Then she started to take slow, careful steps toward the nearby wall, guiding Gianna with careful pressure on her waist.

When Gianna's ass bumped into the wall, she let out a small *oh* that went straight to Megan's crotch. Megan pressed closer to her, her body hungry for the feeling of Gianna's curves. They did not disappoint, soft and yielding and enveloping.

Gianna slid her hand up a little on Megan's head, tangling her fingers in Megan's short hair and pulling her head down more firmly, closer to her mouth. Megan hardly had time to react to that before Gianna's tongue was slipping between her teeth, driving away any rational thought that might have been left.

So she wasn't actually thinking about it when her hands slid from Gianna's sides to her ass, and Gianna made no objection. Megan greedily caressed the full, squishy globes, finding plenty to enjoy there. There was so much of Gianna to explore, and Megan wanted all of it.

But that did seem to be a bit much for the first day they'd met, especially when they were sports rivals. Slowly, rational thought reasserted itself—after some more kissing (though she couldn't characterize it as enough), Megan pulled slowly and reluctantly away.

She and Gianna stared at each other for a few moments, both breathing hard. Megan's skin felt hot all over, and her panties were wet. She'd never met anyone who turned her on this much, this quickly. Was it all just because of that impressive first-jam block?

Gianna's red lipstick was smeared and nearly cleaned off. Megan reached up to touch her lips. Some of that lipstick was probably on her face now.

Gianna's lips curved into that wicked smile again, though with her pupils dilated like they were, the effect was less—or just different. "Well, you look a mess now."

Megan forced herself to laugh. It came out breathy. "Not as much of a mess as your team was after we beat you tonight."

Gianna made a noise somewhere between a grunt and a sigh, then suddenly reached out and grabbed the back of Megan's head again, pulling her down so their lips were crushed against one another. Megan's rational mind told her to back away, but her body was having none of it. She pressed up against Gianna again, both her hands flat on the wall, eliminating any space between them.

Gianna still had a free hand, and she hooked it around Megan's thigh, pulling Megan's leg up so it curled around her—and so Megan couldn't go anywhere until she let go. Megan throbbed everywhere she was touching Gianna and ached everywhere the blocker's hands hadn't yet reached. Her heart was pounding like she was in the middle of a jam, weaving through and shoving past the opposing team.

Now, at least, she understood the attraction. It wasn't just that Gianna was incredibly hot—though that was an important part of it. Megan was into her *because* they were opponents, not in spite of it. The game got their blood boiling, and they had to find someone to take it out on.

This was probably a better way of taking it out than the ones she'd found before.

"So," Shelly said, looking over with a grin as they waited at a stoplight, "how about you and Mountain Bruise?"

"What about us?" Megan said, even though she'd been thinking of practically nothing but Gianna's lips, tongue, and hands since she'd gotten into Shelly's car for the ride home.

"Won't there be a problem on the track if you're dating a member of the opposing team?" Shelly's voice was light and teasing, but Megan still feared that she was seriously worried. After all, Shelly was the team captain—she had to do what was best for the team, and she was good at her job.

Anyway, there was absolutely nothing serious between Megan and Gianna. Just the thrill of the derby rivalry and a pretty powerful physical attraction.

Megan snorted and shook her head. "It's not like that."

"Oh, really?"

"Really," Megan said with a sigh, as though she was tired of being asked about Gianna. "I was just kinda drunk, and she's hot, and available."

"Mm." There were a few moments of silence as Shelly drove fast down the dark, mostly-empty streets. "Maybe a little bit of rebound?"

"Yeah, probably. It had been a while." Megan grabbed happily onto that excuse. Hell, it might even be true. She had, as Shelly and all the girls knew, broken up with her girlfriend a few weeks before. Megan and Cari had been together for three years, and Megan still felt guilty about it—even though she knew she shouldn't. It was roller derby that finally had given her the confidence to give back as good as she'd been getting.

They pulled up in front of the house, a three-story rowhouse where Megan lived in the second floor apartment—above the dancers and below the screaming baby (which was unpleasant, but could have been worse). It wasn't perfect, but it was home. "Thanks," Megan said, unbuckling her seatbelt and climbing out of the car.

When she leaned in through the back door to grab her derby gear, Shelly twisted around to look at her. "You know, getting your giggles in with a rebound partner might not be a bad thing. I know you've been a little messed up. Maybe a clean slate will be just the thing you need to get your head on straight."

Megan laughed, partly at Shelly's comment and partly at 'getting your giggles in,' but mostly to cover up the hurt she felt at Shelly thinking she was messed up. Megan thought she was fine—or at least she thought she was hiding it well.

"What are you doing, being all wise and giving advice?" she teased. "You're what, a year older than me?"

"Hey, as of next month I'll be two years older than you," Shelly said, pointing at her. "And that's two years of valuable life experience, I'll have you know."

Megan shook her head, grinning. "Well, I'll try to keep

it in mind, oh wise and venerable one. See you on Tuesday."
She slammed the car door and headed to her apartment.

CHAPTER 3

It felt like Tuesday took forever to arrive. Megan did spend half the day on Sunday sleeping, then the rest of it eating snacks and watching Netflix, but Monday still came, inexorably, bringing with it her workday.

Her job wasn't all terrible—in fact, some aspects of it were pretty great, mostly the interactions with customers. She worked the front desk at a trampoline park, making reservations, checking people in, and giving them the safety spiel. They got customers of all ages, from two-year-olds just toddling to octogenarians trying to keep up their bone health, and all customers were happy when they came to a trampoline park and bounced around for a while.

Okay, not all of them were happy. There were always a few parents who tried to demand their money back. But

Megan didn't have to deal with any of those that Monday or Tuesday.

What she *did* have to deal with were conflicting directions from her bosses, mysterious charges on the company's bank account (which she managed, but did not have access to use), and at lunchtime on Tuesday, a screaming fight between her bosses, who were husband and wife. Megan had perfected the art of looking perfectly calm and unconcerned during those.

But however calm she might look, she didn't *feel* calm at all, and she was more than ready to spill her adrenaline on some fast skating and some hard blocking.

What she didn't expect was for the team to emerge from the locker room for a few laps of the track and find they had an audience.

Megan was one of the first out of the locker room, so she saw them first. They were on the other side of the track, and she checked her speed as she skated toward them, confused. Were they spectators who'd gotten their dates mixed up? But Monstrous Regiment never had games on Tuesdays—that would be pretty hard to mix up.

As she passed the group, she saw a familiar face at the front. Gianna.

Rolling in the Streets had come to watch them practice.

Anger put a burst of speed on her skates, and she nearly collided with Helen, who was at the back of the pack as the team entered the track.

"Whoa, Splatwood, watch where you're going!" Helen cried.

"Sorry, Helen," Megan said, putting the brake on slightly to match Helen's speed. No one on the team wanted to skate slowly, especially as they warmed up, so they weren't far behind. "I was a little distracted. Did you see our audience?"

Helen's eyes got big as she stared. "What? Our practices aren't interesting enough to have people watching. What are they doing here?"

"Watch as we get close. You'll recognize some of them, I bet." They were passing the first quarter of the track. Megan didn't know which of the skaters Helen might recognize from Saturday's game or afterparty, so she just gestured toward them as a whole.

"What the fuck?" Helen spun on her skates, and Megan had the satisfaction of watching her skate backward, staring at Rolling in the Streets. She was just as shocked and angry as Megan to see them there.

"They can't be here," Helen hissed, spinning again for forward skating. The two of them were catching up with the rest of the pack now.

"I don't know," Megan said. "Are there any rules against it or are they just being colossal jerks?"

"It's got to be cheating," Kristine said, glancing back at their conversation. "Maybe Shelly will talk to them."

As Monstrous Regiment made their next pass, Shelly

did slow down and stop next to the other team. She said something Megan couldn't understand in the big, echoing room, and a dark-skinned black woman (Megan recognized Kiss with a Fist, out of uniform) stood up to talk to her.

"I don't see the problem," Gayle said, matching her speed to Megan's. "It's not like they're going to get any tips from watching us practice. We just do the same kind of thing everyone else does."

Megan rolled her eyes, then turned her head to watch Gianna as they skated around the track. It was impossible to actually recognize Gianna from across the room, but Megan knew where she was sitting. "They can see where our weaknesses are," she said. "What things we're specifically working on."

"Yeah, and they can take advantage of it," Helen said. "You're right, Kristine, seems like cheating to me."

Megan glared at Gianna as they skated past. Now the entire team was talking, muttering to one another. Some, like Gayle, seemed to be unperturbed—Mindy even sounded excited about having another team watching, talking about showing off. But most agreed with Megan that Monstrous Regiment shouldn't be there. At best they were just being obnoxious; at worst they were cheating or even sabotaging the other team.

"How did they even know when we practice?" Tara asked in a low voice—loud enough that only those around her could hear. "A bunch of teams use this track."

Megan happened to be right behind Tara, and her heart

sank. She turned her head as they skated around the track to look at Gianna again.

It was her own fault. Gianna had asked, and Megan had told her. She'd bragged about it. Surely Rolling in the Streets also practiced three times a week or more—but that wasn't the important thing.

It was that Gianna had taken advantage of her, and now her team was paying the price.

Megan put on another burst of speed, weaving past her teammates. They were still just doing laps, not working on a blocking drill, so no one tried to stop her, though she heard a few shouts behind her. She ignored them.

She whipped past Shelly and Kiss with a Fist, who were still talking, at such speed that she knew it looked like she was going to fly right past the rest of the team as well. But she didn't. She stopped hard with the brake on her right skate, making a lightning-fast ninety-degree turn to face Gianna directly.

She was showing off, so she put her hands on her hips and sucked in a breath through her nose, trying to make the move look even more effortless than it actually was. When she had her breathing under control, she glared down at Gianna, who was still sitting on the floor—though at least she'd dropped her shit-eating grin.

"What the fuck is this about?" Megan demanded.

Gianna stared back up at her, unrepentant. "We wanted to watch you practice."

"We?" Megan scoffed. "You mean you tricked our

practice times out of me and snuck into the track while we were changing."

Gianna shrugged. "All's fair in love and derby, babe."

Megan took one skate forward, closing the small distance between her and Gianna. "Love? Don't be ridiculous. You took advantage of me to cheat."

Gianna stood up in one smooth motion, her tits bouncing right up and hitting Megan in the chest. Megan swallowed, her heart pounding for entirely new reasons, but refused to back down. "Don't you care accuse me of cheating," Gianna said, her eyebrows lowering dangerously over her dark eyes. "There's nothing illegal about watching another team practice."

"Yeah, we could—" said one of the girls from behind her, but another one elbowed her and muttered, "Shut up."

Megan barely saw it happen. All her focus was on Gianna. It was only divided between her anger and her desire to slam the other woman against a wall again. Or were they the same desire?

"What do you call this, then? Not cheating, sabotage?" Megan did her best to loom. It should have been easy—she already had five or six inches on Gianna, and she wore skates while Gianna wore flats—but the other woman still had that powerful, indefinable presence that made her seem bigger than she was.

Maybe it was just lust.

"Hey!" Gianna shouted, flinging her hands in the air. "What do you think you're saying?"

"You heard me," Megan shouted back, her blood singing through her veins. This fight was giving her almost as much adrenaline as struggling through a pack of hostile blockers.

Gianna raised her hands and pushed Megan's shoulders, a hard shove that sent her spinning backward for a moment. But she knew what she was doing on skates. She caught her balance and slammed her toe stop down, hearing shouts in the distance. She wanted to tell her teammates she was all right, but all she could focus on was Gianna.

She kicked her skate and brought herself face-to-face with Gianna again. "Do you have a problem with me?" she screamed. "Because I have a problem with you. Get off our track!"

Gianna was answering her question before she could even finish talking. "Yeah, I have a problem with you! How the fuck do you—you don't get to tell me what to do!"

"*Yo!* Calm it down!" Kiss with a Fist had a voice even louder than Gianna's—it cut right through their argument. She seized Gianna by the arm, just as a hand grabbed onto Megan's upper arm.

Megan turned her head quickly, read to swing—or at least to snap—until she saw it was Shelly, glaring at her. "Chill, Megan," she said in her team-captain voice—the one that Megan couldn't help but obey. She loved Shelly, but this time she didn't want to listen.

"Come on," Shelly said, when neither Megan nor Gianna argued. Shelly started skating without letting go of

Megan's arm, and Megan had no choice but to kick off—it was either that or be pulled along bodily on her wheels, which would just be humiliating.

Now that her focus had been moved, she saw that the rest of the team was in a huddle by the locker rooms, whispering to each other but no longer skating. "In the locker room, girls," Shelly called as they skated closer. "I want to talk to all of you."

"You can let go of me now," Megan muttered.

Shelly shook her head. "Not yet." Megan glanced at her, but she wasn't looking at the jammer by her side; she was watching the rest of the team as they filed into the locker room.

Shelly stopped both of them before they had reached the doors. She shook Megan's arm gently, then finally let go. Her dark expression, though, didn't change. "What the hell was that all about?"

"They're cheating. They're here to spy on our weaknesses." It sounded stupid and childish now that Megan said it out loud—or at least now that she said it to Shelly.

"So what if they are? We can deal with it. You didn't need to freak." Shelly frowned, looking at Megan more closely. "I thought you liked that blocker. Mountain Bruise."

Megan swallowed and looked down, forcing herself neither to look at Gianna nor correct Shelly with her real name. "Yeah, I don't know if 'like' is the word."

Shelly snorted, and when Megan looked back up at her,

she was smiling a little. "Okay, but you have to chill, you know?"

Megan took a deep breath and let it out slowly. "Yeah, I know."

Shelly was really smiling now. "Let's talk to the rest of the team."

They skated into the locker room. Half the rest of the team was sitting on benches; the other half was standing around, either fidgeting their skates back and forth or leaning against the wall. Kristine exploded into speech as soon as Shelly entered. "Hey, so are you getting rid of them or what?"

"They're staying to watch our practice," Shelly said. She held up a hand as Kristine, Helen, and a few others started to protest, and the room quieted quickly.

Megan skated over to put her back to a locker, next to Helen. She needed something firm to stand against.

"I talked to their team captain, Janine, and she's right. There's no rule against watching another team practice. In fact, it sounds like it's how some of the best teams work. They just wanted to see how we work, see what makes us tick, because we're so good. I know no one here has forgotten how badly we beat them on Saturday."

Megan snorted. She didn't think it was a compliment that the other team was watching them. But Shelly frowned at her, and she didn't say anything.

"Look, I know it's pissing a lot of you off, but this is

derby, remember? This isn't World War I. No one's going to die if our plans fall into enemy hands."

Mindy guffawed at that, and a few of the other girls snickered. Megan shook her head, but Shelly was right. Derby was competitive when they were skating, but off the track it was usually one big party. What had gotten into her?

Oh, right. Gianna.

Or maybe the problem was that Gianna *hadn't* gotten into her. Yet.

"So take it for the compliment it is," Shelly continued. "And if they see our weaknesses, so what? We're just going to make all of those weaknesses stronger. They might think they see something they can exploit, but there are no cracks in our wall."

"Yeah!" shouted Mindy. A couple of others laughed, but Shelly grinned at her.

"Come on, ladies," Shelly said. "We're better than they are, right?" She gestured for them to cheer, and they did, albeit half-heartedly. Megan couldn't be enthusiastic when she kept thinking about Gianna's gloating face.

"Hey!" Shelly shouted, using her team captain voice again. "Monstrous Regiment is the best! And we're going to cream them on the twenty-seventh just like we did on Saturday!"

This time the cheer was much more enthusiastic, and Megan joined in, raising her fist. That would show Gianna. It didn't matter what she tried to do—Megan, and her team, would still be better than her.

"All right!" Shelly clapped her hands together in front of her chest. "Let's get back out there and show 'em what we got! Three, two one..."

"MONSTERS!" the team shouted, and, cheering, they all skated back out onto the track to drill their hardest.

CHAPTER 4

Megan hung up the phone happily, typing the reservation into the computer system. As usual, she loved talking with customers about the trampoline park—this one had been a boy scheduling a party to follow his bar mitzvah, obviously with his mom in the background giving him advice and being told the prices. He'd been so cute and so excited about bringing his friends to the trampoline park. Megan had been thrilled to help him.

A moment later, she winced when Karen, one of her bosses, came into the reception area. It was never a good sign when they appeared during normal business hours.

Sure enough, Karen was frowning and staring at her phone. "Megan, what's this invoice from Hughes and Taylor? Who are they?"

Megan took a deep breath. How the woman didn't know

this after more than a year in the same business, with the same contractors, she had no idea. "They're the electricians, remember?"

Karen continued to stare at her phone, not even glancing at Megan. "What? Electricians? What work did they do for us?"

Megan refrained from pointing out that the work was clearly spelled out in the invoice. Explaining where her bosses were completely missing something usually did not end well. "It was two weeks ago. Some of the bulbs in the black-light room needed to be replaced, and that room is pretty dangerous with insufficient light."

Karen shook her head, still not taking her eyes off her phone screen. "We can't afford this. What are they charging us so much for?"

Megan sucked her breath in through her teeth and said nothing. She didn't keep the books—she was just a receptionist—but she was pretty sure they could afford the electricians' fee. And if they couldn't afford it, they should have closed down the black-light room and not hired anyone until they had enough cashflow.

And, of course, at that moment Joe, Karen's husband, walked in through the front door—the customer door, not the side door that he had one of two keys to—with a grocery bag over one arm and his hands spread wide. "Hey, hey! Why the long faces? We work at the best place in the world, remember?"

Megan plastered a smile onto her face. "Hi, Joe."

Karen looked up, her expression unchanged. "Joe, the electricians are overcharging us again."

He looked over her shoulder and clucked his tongue. "Karen, honey, it's the same as always. You worry too much. Here, have a beer."

He pulled a beer out of his bag—looked like it was a six-pack in there. Karen took it, her face shutting down as it always did when he criticized her. Megan looked down at her computer. This wasn't any of her business.

She had to look up again, though, when Joe thrust a beer over the top of her monitor. "You have one too, Megs. You look like you're working too hard. This is a fun place."

"Of course it is, sir," she said, summoning up a genuine smile as she remembered the sale she'd just made. "I just booked in a dozen kids for next Saturday night. They're going to be thrilled."

Joe didn't look thrilled—which was odd, because he was generally pretty invested in the business doing well. He leaned over the monitor, putting the beer on Megan's desk, glancing over at Karen as she went into the back room. "Next Saturday?" he whispered. "Don't you have a, you know, the thing?"

Megan stared at him in confusion. She did have a derby game that night—the team had games almost every weekend this time of year—but roller derby had never once interfered with her job, and Joe had always said not to let her job get in the way of her sports prowess.

For that matter, she wasn't scheduled to work on

Saturdays, and she never had been; Joe and Karen ran the place evenings and weekends.

"You didn't want me working then, did you?" she asked. "You know you have to give me more notice than that if you want me to work on a Saturday."

"What? Hell, no! Why would I want you working? I want everyone else out of here. Drink your beer before it gets warm." He tapped it so it rattled on her desk.

"I just brushed my teeth," she lied. "You can put it in the fridge for me."

He didn't seem to hear that part of the conversation, even though he was the one who had initiated it. "Did you not see my note on the calendar? You better not have screwed things up for me."

She could tell he was only restraining himself from shouting with the knowledge that Karen was next door, so she scrolled through the electronic calendar—the only one they used—hastily. There was no note on it. "I honestly don't know what you're talking about."

"What the fuck!" This time he did shout, and he grabbed her monitor in both hands and turned it to face him while she winced away. He breathed heavily while he stared at it, then said in a much calmer voice, "There isn't anything on the thirteenth."

"Uh, no, sir. Nothing booked for that night yet. I just booked for the twentieth."

"Oh. Well, that's all right then." He turned her monitor back to face her, though it was now sitting crookedly. "I don't know what happened to my note. Be sure not to book anything for the thirteenth, all right? I don't want anything else here. Or anyone." He winked.

"Yes, sir. Got it." She tapped it in. That was a close call—it probably wouldn't be long until someone wanted to book that evening. She wished he would communicate better.

"Not going to ask?"

"No, sir." She wouldn't even look at him now. She had no intention of asking him what nefarious thing he was going to be up to in the trampoline park, and she'd rather not think about it at all. She was grateful for the knowledge that she would be in a game that night and unable to think of anything but speed and tactics.

"Good girl. Go on, drink." He tapped the beer again before heading into the back room.

Megan hastily stashed the beer under her desk. She'd bring it home and drink it later—she was never one to turn down free beer, at least if it was still sealed. But she was absolutely not going to drink at work, and it would be even worse to have customers suspect she was drinking at work when she wasn't. If Karen heard that, she would be pissed, and Megan wouldn't exactly look like a responsible receptionist for the customers, either.

She was turning her attention to straightening out her monitor when the door opened, the electronic chime going off to tell her (as if she couldn't see) that it had.

"Welcome to Circle Bounce," she said, then looked up.

At first she didn't recognize the woman sashaying with

confident curves into the room—she just thought that she looked really good in her tight jeans and neat blazer that emphasized her cleavage.

Then her gaze continued up to the woman's face and realized that it was Gianna.

Megan swallowed hard. What could she say? She didn't want to talk about how she knew Gianna—and if Joe heard her acting like she knew a customer, he would be sure to come out and ask. He and Karen were just in the next room. Was the door shut? How well could they hear what was going on in the reception area?

Maybe Gianna just wouldn't recognize her, and she could fake it. That was pretty unlikely, considering Megan's unusually bright hair and nose ring, but there might be a small chance.

Gianna stopped dead in the middle of the room, staring at her.

Okay, no chance at all.

"Megan?" Gianna asked. "You work here?"

Megan plastered on her customer-service smile. It was usually easier to get it to be genuine... but this was a weird situation. "Yes, I'm the receptionist. What can I do for you? Do you want to book a party?" What if Gianna was trying to book the park for Rolling in the Streets? That would be uncomfortable.

Not to mention that fourteen derby girls—all of them powerhouses of muscle, even the short ones like Gianna—would be a bit rough on the trampolines. They were designed to be strong enough for adults, but there were still weight limits.

"Yeah," Gianna said, glancing around as she approached the desk. Was she nervous about who might be overhearing them, too? "I wanted to book a trip for my kids. They do have kids' parties here, right?"

"Uh, yeah," Megan said, her mouth going dry. Gianna had kids? "That's most of our business. How many?"

Gianna leaned her palms on the edge of Megan's desk. Was she deliberately pressing her arms to her sides to emphasize her cleavage? "They have me at twenty-nine right now, but these things tend to shift around a little. Is it okay if you say 'about thirty' and I give you an exact count closer to the date?"

"What?" Megan's hands were poised above the keyboard, but she couldn't type anything yet—her brain was whirring, trying to make sense of what Gianna was saying. "They... shift around?"

"Yeah, up until school actually starts, and sometimes even after that. School doesn't start until the sixth."

A gear finally caught in Megan's brain. "Oh, you're a *teacher*."

"Yeah. Kindergarten." Gianna laughed. "You thought I was a mom? Not yet, babe."

"Okay, so what date are you looking for? During the school day?"

"Yeah. I figure we'll need extra time, with thirty or so

kids. I'll bring chaperones, of course. Some of the parents would be thrilled to come along."

"We do have a rule that every three children must be accompanied by one adult, so for about thirty kids you'll need at least ten adults. They can enter free as chaperones if they're not going to bounce, but if you want to pay for tickets for them as well, the trampolines are open to them." This was easier. Megan knew what she was doing now—customer service.

"Okay, can I just put down a deposit for a date and work out the numbers later? I'm sure some of the parents will want to get on the trampolines, I just don't know how many." Gianna had an odd smile on her face—not the smirk or the triumphant grin that Megan had seen before, but a small, almost tender one. Maybe she was thinking about the thirty tiny faces she would be meeting about a month from now.

"Yes, that's absolutely fine. We do have plenty to appeal to adults—the trampolines are all rated for adult use, and we have gymnastics gear, a basketball hoop, and a newly renovated black-light room."

"Yeah?" Gianna's smile had grown to a smirk now, and she was leaning over, the lapel of her blazer nearly touching Megan's monitor. "I bet you have adult entertainment."

Megan smiled blandly in her face. She was not getting distracted by that expanse of cleavage. No matter how hard she had to work to avoid it. "We have a dress code, of course, and there are no alcoholic beverages permitted on the premises. Everyone can bring one sealed water bottle. It's all laid out on our website, or I can give you a printed brochure if you'd prefer."

Gianna raised her eyebrows, leaning back a little. "No, that's all right, I've been on the website. So what dates can you give me?"

"September during the week is fairly wide open. What day of the week were you looking for?"

"How about Thursday?"

"The eighth is open."

Gianna sucked her teeth. "No, that's too soon. Let's go for October, actually. I need time for them to settle in and get to know me. Especially the parents."

"Sure. October sixth?"

"That sounds perfect."

Gianna looked around the room again while Megan entered the information into the system. "So," she said in a quiet voice, almost whispering, "do you like working here?"

"Oh, I love it." Megan grinned as she finished entering the reservation. "It's the best place I could work. I talk to happy kids, and sometimes adults, every day."

Gianna snorted. "You're lucky. I see happy kids every day, but more often than not they're screaming, snotty, or wetting their pants."

"You don't like teaching kindergarten?" Megan processed Gianna's down payment.

"I absolutely love it. But it's hard. Then again, no job is perfect."

"That's true," Megan agreed. "There, you're all entered in. All you'll need to do is call or email to get the exact details of your reservation in, then pay the balance on the sixth when you come in. And we'll go over the rules with you then, plus get everyone ready and show them how it works. Generally, safety gear is unnecessary, other than our provided socks, but with kids this small we let them bring their own if they want. Do you have any other questions?"

Gianna straightened up, looking at Megan with that odd little smile again, but this time her thick eyebrows were bunched together. "Yeah, how come you're so different at work?"

Megan raised her eyebrows. "It's called being professional."

Gianna burst out laughing. "Okay, there's that snarky Splatwood I've gotten to know. And I'd like to get to know you better. How about it?"

Megan blinked at her, confused. She had not intended her words to be funny or snarky, and now she wasn't sure what Gianna was talking about. She was all off-balance here; her work and derby worlds had never collided before, and she didn't like it.

Gianna leaned forward again. This time she was definitely emphasizing her cleavage. "You and me, Megan. Getting to know each other a little better. What do you say?"

Was she asking her out on a date? That was a terrible idea. She couldn't—

No, she could, Megan reminded herself. There was

nothing to stop her. And why not? Gianna was incredibly hot, and the worst that would happen would be a bland, boring date. If she hated it, then she'd be able to get her mind off Gianna, then channel all her tension back into derby. And if it went well, there'd be some tension there, too.

"Yeah, okay," she said.

"Great!" Gianna flashed a wide white grin that was still different from the others she'd shown Megan. How many smiles did she have?

"What time do you get off work?"

"Five-thirty, but—"

"I know, you have derby practice after work today. I'll pick you up here tomorrow, okay?"

Megan heard noises from the back room. She nodded quickly, swallowing. She definitely did not want one of her bosses to come out and see her getting picked up by a customer. "Sounds great."

"Yeah, I think Friday night is perfect. Plenty of time if we need it, right?" Gianna winked, then turned slowly and sashayed toward the door. Megan wondered if she walked like that all the time or if she just wanted to show off. It was working.

Just as the front door opened, so did the rear door that led to Joe and Karen's office. Megan heard a low whistle, followed by, "Now that is an ass."

"Joe!" Karen shouted furiously. "You can't say that kind of stuff to customers!"

"Come on, Karen," he said, turning around and shutting the door again.

But they were shouting now, and Megan couldn't block it out entirely. She groaned and buried her head in her hands. It was going to be a long day.

CHAPTER 5

By five-thirty on Friday, Megan was more than ready for the weekend. She wished she hadn't agreed to let Gianna pick her up from work; she wanted time to go home, maybe wash her face and apply more interesting makeup than what she wore to work (Joe and Karen liked employing a receptionist with carrot-colored hair and a nose ring, but she didn't want to push that too far), even have a beer so she was a little more relaxed for the date.

But she didn't want to change her plans at the last minute, and anyway, she didn't have Gianna's number. Maybe after tonight that would change.

Megan was surprised at how nervous she was as she packed away her things and headed outside to the parking lot. She kept trying to tell herself that it didn't matter how this date went, but her subconscious wanted to make a good impression anyway. Maybe that was just because it had been so long since she'd been on a first date.

There were only two cars in the parking lot at the moment—Joe's silver convertible and Karen's blue, rectangular SUV. As Megan walked carefully toward the entrance, a little red hybrid pulled into the lot. A party was scheduled for six, but somehow Megan knew anyway that this was Gianna's car.

The car pulled right up next to Megan, and the passenger door opened to reveal Gianna leaning over the seat, her cleavage on spectacular display. "Hey! I didn't mean to make you walk. I'm sorry I was late. You look super cute in that dress."

Megan had meant to reassure Gianna that it was fine, she wasn't more than a minute late, but at the compliment that all dried up to a mumbled, "Thanks." She got in the car awkwardly, unsure how to act. The quiet, mild-mannered receptionist Megan wasn't really her... but neither was foul-mouthed, sassy Margaret Splatwood. At least, not without skates on her feet.

Once she was in the car with the door closed, Gianna drove in a swift, tight circle to get out of the parking lot again. "So, I was thinking it's a little early for dinner, so we'll do something else first. Is that all right with you?"

"Yeah, that's fine. Did you have something in mind?"

Gianna grinned at her. "You bet I do. Hold on tight."

Megan was not at all surprised that Gianna took off driving fast. It fit with her personality—not to mention her car. As she hung onto the handle of the passenger door, she wondered what this exciting date idea was. She hoped it wasn't too exciting. Her muscles were still sore from yesterday's derby practice; she didn't want to do a lot of walking or any other activity.

Gianna took them south and parked at a meter in a popular area of South Philly, where nice houses and university buildings mingled with quirky shops and the occasional empty lot. It wasn't entirely gentrified yet, but there were fun things you could do here. Were they just going to a shop? It wasn't cupcakes, was it? That would seem to defeat the purpose of not going to dinner yet. (Not that Megan would ever say no to cupcakes.)

"Okay, it's a block or two from here," Gianna said. "Come on."

She set a quick pace, obviously assuming Megan was in shape—which true. She might not feel like doing much walking right now, but two blocks was nothing with her derby-trained muscles.

Megan lagged a half-step behind Gianna, both because she didn't know where they were going and because she was looking around at the shops. It had been more than a year since she'd been to this particular street; some things had changed, and most of them for the worse.

But they turned at one particular shop, and that one hadn't changed at all.

"Here we are," Gianna said. "Seemed like the kind of thing you'd like."

Megan couldn't argue with that, not when she was breathing deeply of the aroma and looking around with a useless grin on her face—looking at all the books. She never came here anymore, but she couldn't resist a good used bookstore, and this was a good one.

"Hi, Dusty," Gianna said, leaning her elbows on the counter and talking to the person sitting reading a book behind it. "You have my books?"

"Of course, Gianna," Dusty said, putting down their book and leaning under the counter. "Just like you asked for."

"You must be a regular," Megan commented, impressed and a little jealous at Gianna's rapport with the bookstore worker.

Gianna just smiled. When Dusty emerged, it was with a stack of three hardcovers, tied together with a ribbon.

Gianna took them, turned, and held them out to Megan. "For you. My dad always says, if you want someone to remember you, do something memorable."

"Memorable doesn't necessarily mean good," Megan said, but she still felt her eyes widen as she opened the package. No matter what else happened with Gianna, she wouldn't forget receiving books as a first-date gift.

Her eyes got even wider as she looked at the titles. *Oryx and Crake, The Year of the Flood, MaddAddam*—it was Margaret Atwood's latest science fiction trilogy. Megan had been wanting to read these for ages.

"How did you know I hadn't read these yet?" she managed.

Gianna shrugged. "Lucky guess. I figured even if you had, you might not have this version." She pointed to a sticker on the cover of *Oryx and Crake*. It had been signed by the author.

Megan clutched the books to her chest, grinning. "Wow, if more girls romanced me with books, I'd go on dates a lot more often."

Gianna winked. "I'm smarter than most girls, babe. Do you want to look around the shop or just get going?"

"Let's look around a bit." It was hard not to.

But as Megan perused the titles, eyes skimming over the sideways-aligned words and names, her mind wasn't on them. She was still clutching her gift, and thinking about the kind of person who would give her books—especially a signed Margaret Atwood trilogy.

Gianna had obviously taken to heart Megan's comment that she loved Margaret Atwood. Well, that was easy to remember; her derby name was Margaret Splatwood, after all. It was hard to miss the reference. And that had been only a week ago—they'd seen each other twice more since then.

But still, she and Gianna hadn't been interested in each other when they'd had their brief chat about Margaret Atwood—at least, not any more than physically. Or Megan didn't think so.

They'd only just learned each other's names. Was it possible to become emotionally interested in someone only after seeing them play, not yet getting to know each other?

She still didn't even really know why Gianna was interested in her, but maybe being good at roller derby was as good a reason as any. And Megan was certainly more into Gianna now that she'd gotten the gift.

She glanced through the shelves at Gianna, who seemed to be focused on the books of poetry on that side, her lips twitching slightly as though she were reading the titles softly to herself. What if there was an ulterior motive for this gift? It was pretty extravagant for someone who didn't really know her—they hadn't even started their date. One book would be okay, but three? At least one of them signed by her favorite author?

Megan swallowed and shifted the books in her arms. What if Gianna were just trying to get more information about Monstrous Regiment and its training schedule? She had to know Megan wouldn't give it up willingly, but maybe she hoped she could be persuaded.

It was an awful lot of trouble to go to just to get some information. Practicing harder would be a much better use of Gianna's time. But maybe she couldn't practice harder.

"Hey," said Gianna from right over Megan's shoulder, making her jump. She hadn't noticed the other woman moving.

"Sorry." Gianna took a step back, holding her hands palm-out by her hips as though to ward off an attack.

Megan sucked in a breath and smiled. "It's okay. I was just lost in thought." She wanted Gianna back near her again, but she wasn't going to say that—especially not in a small bookstore, where the clerk could probably hear their every word.

"Did you find something you want?"

Megan shook her head. "You know what, I think three books is enough for today. I don't get a lot of time to read between work and derby practice."

Gianna rolled her eyes heavenward. "I know exactly what you mean. To be honest, I get plenty of reading done, but it's all for six-year-olds. If I don't read another Fancy Nancy book it'll be too soon."

Megan giggled, even though she didn't know what Fancy Nancy was. "I'm sure Margaret Atwood is an excellent antidote."

"Most of the time, yeah," Gianna said with a shrug that used her entire arms. "Anyway, want to head to the restaurant?"

"Sure, did you have somewhere in mind?"

Gianna winked. "It's a surprise."

"If it's the same kind of surprise as the bookstore was, I may not be able to stand," Megan joked.

Gianna grinned fiercely, looking up into her eyes. "Babe, by the end of the night I *definitely* aim to keep you from standing."

Megan's breath caught in her throat. Now was the perfect moment—just lean forward a little bit and lock her lips to Gianna's, those juicy, hot lips. It would be so easy.

But they were in a bookstore, so she swallowed and turned away slightly. "Um, so show me this restaurant."

Gianna led the way back out of the bookstore, saying a quick goodbye to the clerk as they left. Megan added a thank you. The clerk just waved at them lazily, reading their book again.

"You can put the books in the back," Gianna said as they reached her car. Megan checked for traffic, then nestled the books into the seat behind hers, struck for a moment with the absurd idea that she should buckle them in. But they were books; even if Gianna stopped hard and they slid onto the floor, they'd be fine. The dust jackets already had a few nicks from the previous owner.

Once they were both in their seats, Gianna slid the car out into traffic. "It's short for a drive, but too long for a walk. I never want to walk after eating here, anyway—I'm too full."

Megan laughed. "Sounds good." She turned her head to the window and watched the city go by in the bright, late-summer light.

They parked in a garage this time. The blocks around them were more crowded—they were surrounded by tall buildings filled with businesses, a restaurant on every corner. Megan didn't know which one they were headed for.

Gianna took her around the corner to one she hadn't noticed, an elegant-looking Italian place. Megan wondered if she was underdressed, but Gianna was wearing jeans; her dress would probably be fine. "I have a reservation, Sam," Gianna said to the maître d'.

"Of course, right this way," he said with a smile, picking up menus and gesturing them forward. Megan wondered if Gianna knew people all over the city, or if she just took dates to the places where she was on a first-name basis with the staff so she could impress them.

She wondered if Gianna really cared about impressing her.

The table they were seated at was certainly swanky, with a white tablecloth, a real candle, and cloth napkins folded under the silverware. The maître d' set down two menus with a small drinks menu on top and walked away, leaving them to their own devices.

Megan sat down, smoothing her dress under her. Gianna picked up the drinks menu and scanned it. "Do you drink wine at all?" she asked. "I saw you drinking beer at the afterparty."

Megan nodded. "I drink wine sometimes. Beer seems wrong for a place like this."

Gianna grinned, then set down the drinks menu quickly. "Are you all right? You seem nervous."

Was it that obvious? Megan looked down at her bread plate. "I just feel a little underdressed. You didn't tell me we were going anywhere this fancy."

"Hey, you're dressed fine," Gianna said. "Didn't I tell you that you looked great? People don't need to dress up here."

Megan nodded, but she still felt out of place. She reached for the menu and opened it, but couldn't make sense of the words at first.

"Hey, babe." Gianna reached out and touched the back of Megan's hand lightly with her fingertips. Surprised,

Megan looked up. "If you're really uncomfortable, we can leave."

Megan smiled. Oddly enough, Gianna's suggestion made her feel more comfortable. "No, that's okay. You picked this place out, and it seems nice."

Gianna smiled warmly and withdrew her hand. Megan was a little disappointed at the end of the contact, but Gianna picked up the drinks menu again. "So what kind of wine do you like?"

"I don't know." Megan tried to think back to the wines she'd had before, but she'd mostly been drinking them just because they were available; they'd been cheap wines, more about the alcohol content than the flavor. "I don't know anything about wine."

"That's okay. I'll pick something based on what we order. Maybe a bottle, maybe different glasses for each of us. That work for you?"

"Yeah, sure." She hoped they wouldn't work their way all the way through a bottle of wine, but maybe Gianna held her liquor well.

"And order whatever looks good, don't try to pick something cheap, all right? It's on me, and I want you to have a good time, since you've been so kind as to stay here."

Megan laughed. "Hey, I didn't do it to be nice to you. I did it because you said we'd be really full, so the food here must be good."

"Oh, you bet it is," Gianna said, her grin sharpening again. Once Megan returned her attention to her menu,

Gianna picked up her own, and they were quiet for a few moments.

When Megan put down her menu, Gianna asked her what she'd selected; she gave Gianna the names of an appetizer and a pasta dish, to which Gianna nodded appreciatively and ran her finger down the wine list. When the server arrived, bringing them a bowl of bread and glasses of water, Gianna ordered rapidly for both of them, including a bottle of wine with a name so long Megan couldn't even tell how many words were in it.

When the server had left with the menus, Megan raised her eyebrows at Gianna. "I'm a little surprised you didn't order in Italian. You know, go the extra mile to impress me."

"What, *bambina,* you think my Italian is so good? *Grazie mille*, but I did not listen to my *nonna* enough growing up, to my everlasting shame." Gianna accompanied her words—complete with Italian accents on the English words—with exaggerated hand gestures.

They both laughed. "Serves me right for making assumptions about your Italian name," Megan said.

"I could order in Italian, but I'd have to read it. This way was faster." Gianna winked. "My nonna is indeed ashamed of me, but around here they don't care."

The server came with the wine to pour, then set the bottle on the table, between them but by the window. Megan looked at it skeptically. "I hope you're not expecting to get through that whole thing."

"Of course not. But it's nicer if we can both have as much as we want, and I can take home whatever's left in the bottle." Gianna took a sip of her wine, then added, "I'll see how much I can drink based on how much I eat, and whether or not we have dessert. The desserts here are divine."

Megan lifted her own wine glass. "Well, I'll thank roller derby for my appetite, because three years ago I couldn't have eaten a meal and still had room for dessert. Unless they serve really tiny portions here, like at the super-fancy restaurants."

Gianna shook her head. "You think I'd take you to a place where they don't feed you enough? Look at me. And try your wine already. You don't have to like it, but I think you will."

"What, you think you know what my taste in wine is?"

Gianna laughed. "No, I just think it's a really good wine. Try it."

Megan sipped, liking how Gianna hadn't given up on getting her to taste the wine. It was better than the cheap wines she'd had before—richer, with more depth of flavor. She put the glass down slowly, smacking her lips a little to try to figure out the flavor.

"I do like it," she finally said, "but not as much as beer. I'm not sure if I'll finish the glass."

Gianna shrugged, her hands wide. "Fine by me. More for me to take home. Thanks for trying it."

Megan smiled. "Hey, you insisted."

Gianna smiled back at her, and they were quiet for a moment, the restaurant noisy around them but somehow not penetrating. It was just them.

And then the server brought their appetizers, interrupting the moment, but that was okay with Megan. She was hungry.

They ate, swapping pieces of appetizer so they could each try everything. Megan found both delicious. She sipped at her wine some more; she enjoyed it more with each sip, and she hoped that didn't mean that the wine was so strong she was getting drunk.

She was already half full when the main course arrived, and their plates were indeed heaped high with pasta, sauce, vegetables, and—in Megan's case—seafood. She looked at it with mingled excitement and dismay. "You expect me to leave room for dessert after this?"

"The wine will help you digest," Gianna said, pouring her own second glass. "Want me to top you off?"

Megan snorted. "I'm pretty sure that's not how it works." But she let Gianna add a little more wine to her glass.

She took another sip before digging in to her pasta. When she did take a bite, however, she realized quickly that something was wrong. The flavor wasn't what she had expected at all; this was supposed to have an alfredo sauce, and the sauce was thinner, with a strong lemon flavor. It was still tasty, but not quite on the level with the appetizer or the wine—and not what she'd ordered.

She drank some water before taking another bite of the

pasta, just to make sure it wasn't the wine messing with her tastebuds. Before she could finish chewing, Gianna asked, "Something wrong?"

She didn't know how Gianna noticed these things when she wasn't sure herself. "This isn't quite what I expected, is all. It's still good."

Gianna frowned and, without asking permission, stuck her fork in Megan's plate and twirled up some pasta. She chewed it briefly, then shook her head. "No, this isn't what you ordered. I'll send it back."

Megan shook her head quickly. "No need to go to that much trouble. It's still good. I'll eat it."

But Gianna was already lifting her hand in the air, and she snapped her fingers twice, making her whole arm jiggle. In moments, a server was at their table—not the same one who'd served them before. Gianna explained what was wrong, and the server swept the dish away, back to the kitchen.

"You want some of mine while you wait?" Gianna asked.

"Sure, I'll try it," Megan said, reaching over to cover up her embarrassment. She didn't usually like making a fuss like this—not in public. On the other hand, wasn't it Gianna who'd made the fuss, not her? And she kind of liked how Gianna had taken charge of the situation to make sure Megan got what she'd ordered.

"So you're a kindergarten teacher," she said, trying to make conversation. "How'd you end up in roller derby?"

Gianna laughed. "Ruth got me into it. Jane Bowie Knife.

Her son was in my class last year, and we got to talking about it at a parent-teacher conference. She inspired me to try out, and helped me get in, I think."

Megan shook her head. "I don't think you needed help getting in. You're really good." It was weird to her to think of the mom of a kindergartener being the same person as Jane Bowie Knife, but was that really any stranger than Mountain Bruise teaching that kindergarten class?

"That's sweet of you to say. But this was almost a year ago—I've practiced a lot since then. But really, we should talk about something other than derby. We have plenty of chances for that. How do you like working for the trampoline park?"

"Oh, I love it." Gianna had found Megan's second-favorite subject (as long as she could forget about Joe and Karen), and she started telling her all about the different customers she'd had this week, and how excited some of them had been. She didn't even slow down until the server returned with another plate piled high.

"I'm really sorry about that," the server said, sliding the dish in front of Megan. "The chef used the wrong sauce the first time. This one is correct, and the dish is on the house."

Megan started to say that wasn't necessary, then held her tongue; she wasn't the one paying for the meal. Gianna thanked the server and she left.

Megan tried her new dish; it was much better, much more what she'd been expecting. She shoveled some shrimp into her mouth.

"I wasn't sure if you liked your job," Gianna said. "You seemed so nervous when I came in yesterday."

Megan swallowed and tried not to blush. "Uh, I was just afraid my bosses would overhear and realize that I knew you. I might have gotten in trouble for being too friendly with a customer. We're just supposed to get money out of you." She was trying to put a lighthearted spin on her nerves, but she didn't think she was succeeding very well.

Gianna rolled her eyes. "You were the very essence of professionalism. If you got in trouble, I'll go kick their butts."

Megan snorted and promptly had to take a big gulp of water to wash the alfredo sauce back down her throat. "Their *butts*? Oh, right, you're a kindergarten teacher." She felt warmed by the threat, even if it was oddly phrased, even if it wasn't serious. She hoped it wasn't serious. Kicking Karen's and Joe's butts wouldn't solve a single problem in her life and would probably cause a lot more.

"My tongue does loosen a bit playing derby."

"Oh, I noticed that." Megan leered. Gianna snorted into her wine. Oh, good, this time she'd actually managed to get her jokey innuendo to come out right.

She sipped her wine. She hoped it wasn't going to her head too much. "This really is good," she said.

"I noticed that. I'll make a proper wine lover of you yet."

Megan raised her eyebrows. "If you keep plying me with wine, you may get a different kind of lover." Her heart was beating hard. She couldn't believe she was making so much sexual innuendo, especially when she was at least half serious about it. Gianna was gorgeous—she ached to touch her again.

Gianna's teasing smile came out, the lopsided one she'd used when she was flirting with Megan at the afterparty. "Educational purposes only. I would never take advantage of a lady's drunken state."

Megan wasn't sure whether she was serious or not, and didn't want to ask, for fear of what the answer would be. Did that mean that, since Gianna had bought wine, she didn't want to sleep with Megan? Or if she was joking, would that mean she *did* want to sleep with Megan?

Megan was having a good time, but she wasn't sure she wanted to go that far yet.

Okay, parts of her were sure. But her mind and heart needed full trust, whatever her body was saying, and she didn't think she was there yet.

"How are you single?" she managed to ask, even though it wasn't a very good question.

"You're just lucky, I guess," Gianna said with a grin.

"Please," Megan said, scooping up a forkful of pasta. "Maybe if you were getting laid on a regular basis, you'd have less energy on the track. *That* would be lucky for me." She shoved the pasta in her mouth before she could offer to test her hypothesis.

"You wish," Gianna said, making a brushing-off gesture with her hand. "How do we keep getting back on the subject of roller derby?"

"It's my favorite topic. And it *is* how we met."

"All right, what else do you like to do?"

"What else?" Megan asked, surprised enough by the question that she spoke with her mouth half-full of pasta.

"Yeah. In your free time." Gianna smirked. "You know—Mondays, Wednesdays, Fridays, and Sundays, after work when you're not practicing roller derby? And don't say go on dates, because you were way too surprised when I asked you out for this to be a regular occurrence for you."

Megan swallowed, trying to think of an answer to Gianna's question. What did she do? It had been dates, for a while—or, more often, staying home in the evenings with Cari. But she didn't live with Cari anymore, she was safe, and at the moment she couldn't remember at all what she did with her time on those days off.

"Uh, you know, the usual," she said.

"The usual what?"

"Beer. Netflix. On Sundays I'll usually go grocery shopping, make my lunches for the week. Sometimes I actually clean."

"You don't have any hobbies?"

Megan shrugged. "With roller derby, who has the time? What about you?"

Gianna sighed and lifted her wine glass in a mock toast. "You got me. Between roller derby and teaching, there isn't really time for anything else."

"You can't have homework to grade."

"Rarely, but I have to plan my lessons, keep in touch

with parents, do professional development—there's more to keep up with than you'd expect."

"I don't believe you." Megan glanced down at her plate, wondering if she dared shove more into her face. It was delicious, but she had to stop if she wanted room for dessert. "It's summer. You told me yourself that school doesn't start for a couple more weeks. What do you do with your time?"

"Ask pretty girls out on dates."

Megan rolled her eyes. "Are we getting dessert, or should I eat another bite?"

"Dessert. I'm desperate for their salted caramel pudding. I'm surprised you want to change the subject." Gianna rested her elbows on the table and her chin on her hands, leaning forward as though interested in what Megan had to say. It was probably just a coincidence that it framed her incredible depth of cleavage so well.

"You don't want to answer the question."

"You gave up quickly. It's not like you."

Megan crossed her arms. "How do you know what's like me and what isn't?"

"You never give up when it comes to roller derby."

"And I thought you asked me on this date to try to figure out the paradoxes in my personality. I never promised to make it easy for you."

Gianna laughed a wonderful guffaw, then turned to the server, who had managed to time her appearance perfectly. "Salted caramel pudding and two spoons, please."

"Of course," said the server. "Do you want these boxed to go?"

"Yes, please," Megan said. Gianna nodded, and the server took both dishes.

Gianna pushed the top of the cork down into the wine bottle. "I guess we'll just have to go on another date, then, so that I can unpack your personality a little bit more."

"I guess we will," Megan said, her heart pounding again. She didn't know if she was doing the right thing. But a second date couldn't hurt any more than the first one had, could it? And the only thing this date was hurting was the elasticity in her stomach.

"How about a picnic lunch on Sunday? I'll pick you up and we can sit in the park if the weather's nice. You can make us sandwiches or something."

"Do you always take charge like this?"

"When I know what I want, I go for it." Gianna lowered her head, looking at Megan with intense, dark eyes that seemed to bore into her. "And I want what I see right now."

Megan's mouth went dry. She had no idea what to say to that. She liked Gianna's straightforwardness—she liked the way she took charge. But it made her nervous at the same time. She knew that she should be taking charge of her own destiny, making her own decisions, but it was impossible to resist Gianna.

This was still making her own decisions, though, wasn't

it? She was making a decision to continue dating Gianna. To see where it went.

"I still think this is strange," she said, the words flowing out of her in a rush. "Just sitting together like this. Not trying to compete with each other."

"How many of your dates have been competitive?"

Megan shook her head, trying to dislodge memories. Cari had never been competitive; she hadn't needed to. "That's not what I mean. It's not because we're on a date, it's because we're on opposite teams."

"I thought that was what made it fun."

"Oh, it is." Megan remembered playing against Gianna on the track, trying to get past her, but instead slamming into her curvy body over and over. She also remembered making out with her after the game. She wasn't sure which was better.

The server set down the pudding on the table between them, with two spoons beside it. Megan and Gianna both reached for their spoons at the same time. Their fingers touched—and they'd touched before, but the unexpectedness of it, this time, sent electricity arcing up Megan's fingers to her spine.

Her breath caught in her throat and she jerked her hand back. She wanted that feeling again, but she was afraid of it. And she didn't understand why she should fear it; she'd touched Gianna plenty of times.

Gianna picked up one of the spoons and offered it,

handle-first, to Megan. "Here, babe, you should try it first. I've had it before."

Megan took the spoon nervously, making sure her fingers didn't touch Gianna's this time. Gianna seemed to be watching her as she dipped the spoon into the pudding in its glass cup.

As she brought the spoon to her mouth, she could see that Gianna was definitely watching her. Her cheeks warmed, and she tried to eat her bite of pudding off the spoon in a normal way, not putting any sexual spin on it. She wasn't sure if she succeeded, from the way Gianna's eyes brightened.

The moment the pudding hit her tongue, though, she forgot that Gianna was watching her at all, sighing inadvertently with pleasure. It was delicious, hitting the perfect spot between the bite of the salt and the cloy of the sugar. There was some weight to it, some texture, but mostly it slid down her throat with no resistance at all.

She eagerly attacked the cup again, scooping up a bigger spoonful this time. "This is delicious," she said. "You'd better get some before I eat it all."

Gianna laughed and picked up the other spoon. "I told you to leave room for dessert."

"You may have to roll me out of here, but I have room. I'm just glad I didn't wear jeans today."

"Mine are stretchy," Gianna said with a wink. "They have to be, to make it over my ass."

“It’s worth the trouble,” Megan said, then stuffed her mouth with pudding again.

“There’s the derby girl I met las week,” Gianna said, pointing at her with the spoon. “Maybe it’s just my ass that inspires all the sass.”

Megan shook her head, keeping her mouth shut even though the pudding was mostly gone. This food didn’t last long enough.

The server came with their boxes and the check, which Gianna paid without looking at it. Megan tried not to raise her eyebrows at that. Presumably, Gianna came here a lot, so she already had a sense of what the prices were like. But—

“Don’t you want to at least check that my entrée was free, like they said?” she blurted.

Gianna’s eyebrows lifted a fraction, making her nose look long and Roman. “Why? I trust them to tell me the truth.”

“I just thought... you’d want to make sure. You come here a lot, though, don’t you? You seem to know people.”

Gianna smirked. “It’s a family thing. My dad’s cousin is the owner. I doubt he’s here today, but my parents would probably have told him I was coming.”

“Oh.” Megan looked around the restaurant, curious now. Gianna was related to someone who owned something this fancy? “You have connections, huh?”

“Dusty isn’t related, if that’s what you’re thinking. I just go to the shop a lot. They have good books for my classroom, and for me to take a break from kindergarten stuff.”

"Oh, that's what I figured. This place just seems really fancy. Does your family have money?"

"They're well-off, mostly. Not super rich. My parents spoil me a little." Gianna shrugged broadly. "A place like this runs pretty tightly, but my dad's cousin owns three or four restaurants, I think. You're not accusing me of mob connections, are you?"

Megan grinned. "Please. If you had that, you could just threaten your way into winning every derby game."

"That would take all the fun out of it." When Gianna's card came back, she pocketed it and stood up, stretching her arms over her head. Megan decided that staring at the curves and ripples of her body was not rude—Gianna had asked her out, after all.

Gianna finished her stretch, grinned at Megan, and held out her hand. "Ready to get out of here?"

It *was* getting late. Megan scraped the last tiny bit of caramel pudding out of the cup and let Gianna help her up. Her hand was warm and firm, and she was strong, pulling Megan up without much help—not a surprise.

They took their food and headed toward the entrance. The sky outside was dark. The maître d' and Gianna nodded to each other as they left.

Gianna took in a deep breath of the warm summer air. "Only a couple more weeks of relaxation like this. Then the school year starts again."

"You can always do stuff on a Friday night, can't you?" Megan asked.

"Yes, but I can't relax as much. I always think about the prep I could be doing. Oh, well." She threw Megan a teasing grin. "Only thirty-seven more years and I'm eligible for a nice, cushy pension."

Megan thought of her own puny 401(k) match and grinned back. "Maybe I should marry you. That gets me the pension even if you die, doesn't it?"

"Please. You think you'd be able to get away with that?" Gianna elbowed Megan lightly in the side, then started walking back toward the car.

"I could make it look like an accident." Megan could keep up with Gianna easily—her legs were practically twice as long. "Especially if you keep playing derby. Oops, I accidentally kicked you into a wall."

"You couldn't kill me that way. I'm resilient. You see this?" Gianna slapped her chest. "Protective padding."

Megan stared at Gianna's chest even more blatantly than she had been before. "Is that what it's for? Could've fooled me."

"It helps with getting pretty girls to go out on dates with me, too." Gianna unlocked the car, and Megan slid into the passenger seat, holding her still-warm leftovers in her lap.

Talking with Gianna was easier when she didn't think so hard. She just riffed off whatever Gianna was saying, even if she didn't mean it, and she hoped Gianna didn't, either.

Of course, now that she'd noticed that, she was tongue-tied again. Gianna started the car, and they sat in silence as she maneuvered back into traffic. The lights of the city were coming on as the day darkened.

"I hope that awkward silence doesn't mean I did anything wrong," Gianna finally said.

Megan swallowed. "Nope. Sorry, it's just me. I'm awkward."

"You don't seem awkward to me."

Megan shook her head, though she didn't know if Gianna could see her movement very well. "I know what I'm doing when it comes to derby. The rest of the time? I'm just flailing about. Besides, I contain multitudes, remember?"

Gianna laughed. "Sure, Walt. Speaking of which, where am I taking you?"

"Uh, definitely not over the bridge. Right direction, though. I live in Northern Liberties."

"Oh, okay. Let me know where to turn when we're getting close." Gianna accelerated, changing lanes, but had to put the brakes on almost immediately at a red light.

"Wow, you're a lot less convenient than an Uber. They always know where they're taking me."

Gianna snorted. "But they don't feed you. You don't have your own car?"

"Never felt the need. The bus gets me to work and the El gets me to derby. Other people's cars get me a lot of places, too. Also, I'm paying off my student loans a lot faster without a car payment on top of it."

"Damn, smartypants. I wish I was as smart as you."

Megan laughed a little. "I work at a trampoline park and you're a teacher. I think you're a lot smarter than me."

"Maybe I am. My loans are getting forgiven, as long as I stick with this school. The car loan, though, no way."

"Well, as long as you're not racking up credit-card debt, I think we're both doing pretty well."

"Derby broke me of my shopping habit. Now I only buy what I need, because I get my kicks on skates instead."

"Me, too!" Megan was oddly surprised—had she and Gianna really had the same addiction, shopping to suppress other needs? She just hoped they didn't have the same ex-girlfriend, which could get really awkward. "I used to buy a new dress or three every month, but now I can't believe how full my closet is."

"PMS shopping?"

"Uh, yeah." That was an oversimplification—and it hadn't been Megan's cycle that had driven her to shop. But she didn't want to get into her history with Gianna. Not now, maybe not ever. She was having fun, but that wasn't the same thing as spilling all her secrets.

Luckily, she was able to change the subject by giving Gianna directions to her apartment. Soon they were pulling up in front of it. The lights were on bright on the first floor; the dancers were having another party. "Nice house," Gianna commented.

"Thanks. I just have the second floor." Megan bit her tongue before explaining that she lived alone. She didn't want Gianna to take that as an invitation to come inside.

Of course, if Gianna was the one to suggest it, she didn't think she could say no. But right now, she was not ready to be the one to make the first move.

Gianna did put the car in park and unbuckle her seatbelt, but what she said was, "Let me grab your books for you."

Megan got out awkwardly, fishing for her keys while holding her leftovers, and Gianna moved quickly around the side of the car, retrieving the books from the back seat. She handed them over to Megan, but kept hold of them briefly. "You're really happy with the books?"

Megan couldn't help smiling. "Of course. They're an amazing present. I don't know when I'll have time to read them, especially if we're going on a picnic on Sunday, but I'll find it somehow."

"Bring them on the bus."

Megan nodded. "That's probably what I should do." She was nervous about bringing a book signed by Margaret Atwood on public transportation, for fear of losing it, but she knew that was irrational. She always had her phone out on the train, and she hadn't lost that yet.

"Great," Gianna said. "Then have a good evening, and I'll see you on Sunday, because we're playing the Bottoms-Up Babes tomorrow night and I can't come see your game."

Megan laughed, a strange joy bubbling up in her that she couldn't repress. They'd both be playing derby tomorrow night, going all-out, probably not thinking of each other at all. And yet they'd be doing the same thing. "I hope you wipe the floor with them."

She thought Gianna would wish Monstrous Regiment good luck in their game as well, but she didn't.

What she did was put one hand on the back of Megan's neck, pull her head down, and deliver a kiss that left her dizzy, breathless, and completely overwhelmed.

"Good night," Gianna said, heading back to the car before Megan could entirely recover. Megan walked to the door of her building, put her key in the lock, and looked back. Gianna was sitting in the driver's seat of her car, looking at her. She blew a kiss, then drove off.

Smiling and shaking her head, Megan climbed the stairs to her apartment. She didn't know what she'd gotten herself into, but she liked it.

CHAPTER 6

Megan pulled her skate laces tight, grinning as she did. Tonight was the night: they were playing Rolling in the Streets again, and Monstrous Regiment was better than ever.

"Ooh, that's an evil smile," Shelly said, grinning back at Megan as she walked by on her usual pre-game check of all the girls. "I like your attitude. Ready to defeat Mountain Bruise again?"

Megan nodded, though she felt her smile fade a little. She'd seen Gianna four times now since the last match—once at work, followed by three dates. She definitely wouldn't qualify things as serious, and scorching kisses was as far as they'd gotten, but saying nothing to Shelly still felt a little like lying.

She hadn't told any of the other girls that she was actually dating Gianna now. She wasn't trying to keep it a secret—okay, maybe she was keeping it a secret from Shelly, just because of the advice she'd been given two weeks ago. But she just didn't know how to bring it up. How did she explain that she was going out with someone on the opposing team?

No one seemed to notice her nerves, and the team met up together in the middle of the locker room the way they always did. Shelly gave them a little pep talk, they screamed, and then they were skating out onto the track, having their derby names shouted by the announcer. Megan felt her body flood with adrenaline.

The teams circled each other; she and Gianna sent each other fierce grins. No one but them had any reason to think they were smiling for any reason other than the anticipation of winning. In fact, Megan wasn't sure that she was smiling for any other reason. Just because she liked Gianna didn't mean she wasn't ready to smear the floor with her.

Megan wasn't playing in the first jam—that was always frustrating, but Monstrous Regiment had the full complement of fourteen skaters, and with only five on the track at any one time, it was pretty much impossible for the same jammer to start off every game. Besides, Shelly kept saying that Megan would injure herself if she played in too many jams.

Watching on the sidelines was always frustrating, but today's game was even worse than usual. Jane Bowie Knife, the jammer for Rolling in the Streets, pulled ahead almost immediately, quickly making lead jammer and then racking up the points. She even got past Sir Blocksalot twice. Megan was almost yelling herself hoarse.

She wasn't in the next jam, either, but at least Helen—Jane the Ripper—made lead jammer this time. She couldn't make up for the lead that Rolling in the Streets had on them, though.

Finally, in the third jam, Megan was on. She rammed on her helmet and skated onto the track with unnecessary force, rolling past Mary Read at the jammer line and having to skate backward to be in position in time for the jam to start. She gave Mary—she recognized her now—a scowl, which was returned as a sickly-sweet smile.

They lined up together, the blocker pack ahead of them, waiting for the whistle. Megan's heart was beating double-time. She was ready for this.

She was onto her second stride before the whistle blast even ended, powering down the track toward the blockers. They had to move more slowly; they had to stay together. All she had to do was get past them. She was going to blast right through.

And then Gianna was there, throwing her gorgeous ass in the way, bouncing Megan straight backward. For a moment Megan felt furious betrayal. How could Gianna block her after all that time together?

Then Gianna licked her lips tauntingly, and a wave of lust passed up and over the fury. If this hadn't been derby, her favorite thing in the world, she would have grabbed Gianna right then and there.

But it *was* derby. And part of derby was the competition. Luckily, this had all taken place in seconds, and she regained her composure before Mary Read had actually caught up.

She would skate *around* Gianna this time. And that's what she did, passing her by, then figure-eighting around the other three jammers on the team. Killy Kelly nearly got her with an arm, but Megan slipped past her without even touching.

She raised her fists to acknowledge the cheers from the crowd. She was lead jammer now; the jam was under her control, and she could end it when she wanted, or keep going until time was up.

She almost never ended a jam.

Megan picked up speed again, aiming for the back of the pack. Mary Read had gotten through the pack, past all four Monstrous Regiment blockers, but she wouldn't be racking up points until her next time around. Megan slipped past Britney Scares with a clever fake—but then found herself blocked by Gianna again. This time she bounced off her tits.

Megan bit her lip. She didn't know if Gianna was doing it on purpose or not, but it seemed that they just couldn't stop running into each other. Gianna never blocked with her arm or her leg; she always seemed to go straight for the ass and the chest.

Of course, they were the biggest, softest targets.

Megan tried to get past her again and again, but she just couldn't get up the speed or momentum to go around

Gianna. Gayle tried to get her out of the way, but even Gayle's bulk couldn't move Mountain Bruise.

And it wasn't just the roller derby that was frustrating Megan now. Every time she touched Gianna, her skin tingled a little more. She wanted to grab her—either to pull her close or push her away—but hands were against the rules; that could get her a penalty, and the last thing she wanted was to be off the track.

Finally, though, she managed to give Gianna a shove with her upper arm, right in the chest. It was enough to send Mountain Bruise just a few inches out of the way, and gave Megan room to skate past.

Gayle got her through the rest of the pack, moving the opposing blockers aside, and she made it out past them and to another round again.

It wasn't any easier to get past Gianna the third time, and in fact, she didn't—the jam ended before she could make another full pass. But now that no more points were being scored until the next jam, she could goose Gianna a little—just a light pat to the back of her thigh—and no one was the wiser. Except Gianna.

When Megan sat back down on the bench, she was hot and panting for more than one reason. She was glad to have the excuse of the physical exercise, grabbing a bottle of water and guzzling down half of it. "Damn," Helen said, leaning over to her as they sat to wait out the next jam. "You and Mountain Bruise really have it in for each other, don't you?"

"I don't have anything against her," Megan said.

"That's not really what I was thinking," Helen said, but she didn't push it.

The next jam went just as badly as the first. Or, if you were Rolling in the Streets, it went just as well. They definitely seemed to have improved since the last match; Megan wondered if they really had picked up tips somehow from watching Monstrous Regiment's practice. She didn't think it was that her team was playing badly—they were just as fast and ferocious as ever.

In Megan's next jam, Gianna wasn't blocking. This time she really racked up the points. But she wasn't playing in most of the jams, and she couldn't quite catch Monstrous Regiment up to Rolling in the Streets.

Of course—of *course*—she and Gianna were both playing again in the final jam of the match. Megan bit her lip and gritted her teeth. She'd been going too easy on Gianna earlier. They liked each other too much, that was the problem. She was going to have to stop thinking about her generosity and luscious body, and just see her as another derby player.

But this time seemed to be even worse. Megan was determined to bring the points up, and she wouldn't have too much trouble getting past the other blockers, but Gianna would be there again and again. She started to wonder whether Gianna had said something to the team—"Margaret Splatwood is mine."

It wouldn't be too far from the truth.

Megan got past her twice, but she always had to come back around, and there was Gianna, pressing soft flesh into her, throwing her off-balance, sending her skates sideways or backward. Megan started to lose her concentration.

She looked Gianna straight in the eye. This was getting to be unbearable. Every touch inflamed her nerves. She needed to get Gianna's clothes off, and soon—but first they had to get through the match.

She slowed her skates. Gianna looked confused, obviously not guessing her tactic. Megan couldn't get too far from the pack, but she could move away from them a little bit. With everyone else going forward as fast as they could, the space opened quickly.

Gianna was still watching her, taking swift glances over her shoulder, obviously not wanting to lose track of her position. She thought she knew what Megan was doing. But Megan had a plan—probably a stupid plan, because she'd never practiced it before, but she was sure that was the only thing that could make it work.

She kicked her skates back into action, getting speed, faster and faster. She aimed straight for Gianna. Gianna turned to skate backward, grinned at her, and got low, crouching toward the ground—just what Megan was hoping for.

She couldn't have done it without the speed. She kicked up and leapt into the air, soaring straight over Gianna and landing cleanly on her other side. Her momentum took her right past the other blockers. The crowd was roaring. And then the jam ended.

Unfortunately, derby teams didn't get extra points for spectacular passes. The match still ended with Rolling in the Streets the victor, 47 points to 42.

Megan could hardly focus on the loss. Her skin still felt like it was buzzing. When the teams made their final lap, she caught Gianna's eyes again and touched her tongue to her upper lip. Gianna returned a tiny nod. Megan just hoped they were giving each other the same signal.

Back in the locker room, the players were all buzzing, going over the match aloud. Some people, like Megan, were mad they'd lost; others, like Tara, had just thought it was fun, a great game. It had been really good, Megan was forced to admit.

"Want a ride?" Shelly asked her as they all changed into normal clothes. "We're going to a dance club this time. You look like you need to burn off a little more adrenaline."

"No thanks," Megan said, tossing her gear into her bag. "I'm just going to go right home."

"Oh, come on, just because we lost is no reason to be upset about it. You had fun at the last afterparty, didn't you?"

Megan shook her head. "Maybe a little too much fun. Look, I'm not pissed, I swear. I'm just tired. I've had a long week." She stood up.

Shelly shrugged, obviously disappointed, but not arguing anymore. "If that's what you really want."

"It is." She was only half lying. She did intend to take Gianna directly home.

Sure enough, when she got out back, Gianna was waiting for her.

"You fucking cheated," Megan said. Lust was boiling up in her at the sight of the curvy blocker, but the anger came right up with it. "I can't prove anything, but I know, and you know I know."

"Shut up," Gianna said, grabbing her face and kissing her with no other hesitation.

Megan held on, keeping Gianna close as the wet heat of her mouth washed over her. It felt so good, this attraction, even though they hated each other half the time. Maybe that was *why* it felt so good.

As Gianna's knee pushed between her thighs, it struck her what she was doing.

She'd found another woman, bold and demanding, strong and powerful. Just like Cari. Except this time Megan was strong and bold right back.

She wasn't going to let herself get knocked around again. This wasn't asking for someone exactly like Cari, the same dynamic all over again with another person. This was new; this was healing.

She was just using Gianna as a surrogate, a way to finally get out all her anger at Cari. She knew that Cari wasn't going to hurt her again, but she still needed to convince her brain of that, and making sure she had power in a relationship was a good way to do it.

Maybe it wasn't healthy, but it sure was fun right now.

"Your place or mine?" Gianna breathed into her ear, making shivers run up and down her spine.

"Mine," Megan said. She was going to keep the power in this relationship. "Come on."

Gianna had to park several blocks away from Megan's apartment, but that didn't slow them down one bit. It was dark, and no one was going to give a second look to two women stopping between street corners to make out.

They did, however, finally reach Megan's apartment, and she unlocked the door and led Gianna up the single flight of stairs. They dropped their derby bags at the entryway and she turned on the lights.

"This is a seriously adorable place," Gianna said, looking around.

"Shut up," Megan said, deliberately echoing her from earlier, but instead of kissing her, grabbing her by the hand and pulling her toward the bedroom.

Gianna followed willingly, even giving Megan a push when they reached the foot of her bed, so that she sat down on it abruptly. Gianna immediately climbed into her lap, straddling her and reaching for the hem of her shirt. Megan let her take the shirt off, but once she had her hands free again she reached greedily for Gianna's top, peeling it from her ample flesh.

Gianna was already going for Megan's bra, rushing,

pushing her way to be first. Megan didn't care. She just wanted to release Gianna's breasts from the impressive feat of engineering holding them up.

Finally, Gianna's flesh spilled into Megan's hands, just at the same moment as Gianna's small, fleshy hands covered Megan's own, much smaller chest, caressing the flesh and tweaking the nipples. Megan let out a loud, involuntary moan, jerking her hips forward. She hoped the obnoxious neighbors could hear her.

She tried to push Gianna over, lay her down on the bed where she could get a better look at her body, but Gianna resisted, holding them both in place with her powerful thighs. Instead, Megan tried to content herself with kneading Gianna's heavy breasts between her hands, weighing them and squeezing them, enjoying their warm softness and their impressive heft.

It wasn't enough. She reached down for the waistband of Gianna's leggings and slid them down over her ass. The way Gianna was straddling her, she couldn't get the fabric down any further, but at least now she could get a proper feel of the luscious flesh that had been taunting her all night.

As Megan's hands sank into the wonderful softness of Gianna's ass, Gianna gasped, lifting up on her knees slightly and bending forward so that her chest pressed against Megan's. "Oh, babe," she murmured. "You don't have to..."

"Shh," Megan said, squeezing her ass still harder. She flicked one finger down to stroke Gianna's lower lips. She was wet—but not wet enough, not yet. Not as wet as Megan felt herself to be.

Then Gianna's hands were on the waist of her pants, pushing them and then pulling down past her narrow behind and bony hips. Gianna slipped from Megan's grasp and down between her legs. Megan tried to stand, but Gianna pushed her feet to the side so that she couldn't get her balance. Her shoes came off, then her pants and underwear, and Gianna tossed it all to the side.

Megan tried to haul Gianna back up onto the bed with her, but Gianna still wouldn't let her have her own way. She lifted her head only long enough to suck on Megan's right nipple, so hard that she moaned aloud again, her hands tightening to grip the duvet.

Then her lips went lower, suckling at Megan's labia, then nuzzling between. Megan groaned out loud, sweat bursting out all over her overheated skin. "Gianna..."

"Just lie back, babe," Gianna whispered, her breath tickling Megan's skin so that she shivered all over. "I know what I'm doing."

"Oh, I believe it," Megan said, her voice coming out breathy and shaky. But with Gianna's damp breath washing over her most secret parts, it was amazing she could even talk at all.

"You calling me a slut?" Gianna said, sliding her hands up Megan's thighs. "Because I am." She pushed the tips of her thumbs between Megan's labia.

Megan gasped, her breath shuddering in her throat. "No way. I don't believe it."

"Believe me, babe." Gianna's thumbs worked their way in, sliding between Megan's slick folds, pushing into her throbbing hole. "I've been with a lot of other women."

"Why would you even tell me that?" Megan pushed her thighs apart a tiny bit more, giving Gianna more space to work.

Gianna's dark head moved forward, and then her lips were on Megan's clit, just resting there, not pressing or sucking. "I just want you to know where all this comes from." Her lips fluttered against Megan's sex, sending jolts of pleasure through her.

Then she started to put more pressure on, light at first, then harder and harder. Rolling waves of pleasure crashed through Megan's body. Even if she'd wanted to hold back her cries, she couldn't. Her body was uncontrollable with ecstasy.

The only thing she could do of her own will was hang onto the edge of the mattress—and stare down at Gianna's luscious body. From here, she could see the dip at Gianna's waist and the vast curve of her ass, and it made her mouth water.

Then her vision blurred as Gianna's tongue came into play, teasing, lapping at her clit. She felt pressure inside her vagina—Gianna's thumbs were pushing inside.

Megan's cry broke in the middle, as she pushed herself

further forward, harder onto Gianna's lips and hands. It didn't seem to faze her lover. She felt Gianna's tongue pressing hard against her clit, and all her muscles started to shake.

Then Gianna pulled back a little bit, her face appearing out of Megan's crotch, that familiar smirk on it. Megan shivered. "Don't stop," she begged.

"It's better this way," Gianna whispered, the slight vibrations in the air from her voice tickling Megan's sensitive nerves. "Don't you think?"

Megan shook her head. Anxiety was coiling in her stomach. "Please don't stop. Please." Had she lost control so soon? Maybe this wasn't fun anymore.

But Gianna listened to her, her lips returning to Megan's sensitive nub, one thumb sliding out of her so the other could push further in. Megan screamed out loud and threw her head back. Gianna was sucking so hard that it almost hurt. Megan couldn't control her muscles.

Finally, her orgasm exploded through her, making all her muscles seize up at once. She couldn't breathe for the intensity of the pleasure. Gianna had found some sensitive spot inside her and was pressing her thumb hard against it, and the orgasm kept rolling and rolling until it finally petered out, leaving Megan sweaty and exhausted.

She fell backward onto the bed, trying to catch her breath. Gianna crawled up onto the bed next to her, grinning that cat-that-ate-the-canary grin again.

The smile annoyed Megan. Gianna thought she'd won

again, didn't she? Well, Megan was going to show her otherwise.

She had more energy, even after a derby match and an orgasm, than she'd had a year ago. Her muscles were already back up to strength. She sat up, pushed Gianna's shoulder to lay her back on the bed, and plastered her mouth to Gianna's, devouring the heat and softness of her lips, with the taste of Megan's sex still on them.

Gianna let out a tiny whimper, straight into Megan's mouth, and Megan felt a surge of adrenaline and pleasure. She was in control now. She was the one making Gianna feel good.

She slid her hands down Gianna's body, relishing the curves of her breasts and belly, the thick shape of her thighs, and then the softness of her mound. She still had panties on, and Megan pulled their mouths apart to investigate that.

She remembered now that she'd only pulled Gianna's underwear down, not off. She rubbed the front of the cotton fabric, then slowly slid her fingers down and up the crotch. It was wet, the fabric dragging against her fingers. Gianna let out another little whimper, her thighs twitching. Her eyes were closed.

"Gianna," Megan said. Gianna opened her eyes again, and they locked gazes, Megan still sliding her hand up and down Gianna's crotch. "Tell me what you want."

"Megan..." Gianna's breath caught. She didn't seem to be able to speak any more than that.

Her breasts were jiggling with every breath. Megan devoured her with her eyes. Gianna was so beautiful she could hardly stand it. She wanted to make her come.

"Is this what you like?" Megan coached her. "Or do you want more?"

Gianna bit her lower lip and nodded. Megan would have liked to tease her more, but that little bite was so sexy that she couldn't bear it.

She took hold of Gianna's panties and pulled them down, sliding them over her thighs, her calves, and finally her feet so she could drop them on the floor. Then she slid her hands back up the smooth skin of Gianna's legs, between her thighs, and pushed them apart to expose her sex, shining with moisture.

Megan was glad she kept her nails trimmed short as she slid two fingers into Gianna's inviting opening. Gianna cried out, her legs pushing at the air but finding no purchase. Her muscles squeezed tight around Megan's fingers, but there was so much liquid lubrication that Megan easily slid in and out.

"Do you like this?" Megan whispered, and Gianna nodded hard.

She had room, so she slipped a third finger in, thrusting harder. Gianna gasped and clutched at the sheets. Her eyes were closed again. Megan didn't know whether to tell her to open them or not; she liked the idea that she was giving Gianna so much pleasure that she had to close her eyes to concentrate on it.

She lifted her other hand to Gianna's nub and stroked around it at first, feather-light touches that become stronger and firmer as her hands became wet with Gianna's fluids. She circled it, then came closer and closer until she was pressing right where it emerged from the pubic bone.

Gianna was moaning and panting, her breath coming in gasps. She was sweating at least as much as Megan had. Her nipples, hardened to tight points, drew Megan's eyes as her breasts bounced. Megan leaned in and sucked on one. It was full and hot in her mouth; she slid her tongue over it with relish.

Her fingers slipped lower on the shaft of Gianna's clit, stroking where the sensitive nerves emerged from the hood, and Gianna let out a high keen. But to Megan's surprise, she curled her knees up, pushing them against Megan's arm as though she meant to protect her crotch. "Not there," she gasped. "Too much."

"Oh—uh—sorry." Megan's cheeks burned as she pulled her hands away, and she was glad now that Gianna had her eyes closed. She looked at her fingers, practically dripping with Gianna's fluids. Now what?

Gianna sat up, pushing herself up on her elbows and blinking her eyes open. "Come on, Splatwood, you've got momentum. Don't stop now. Just be a little more gentle." Her smile was lopsided and utterly gorgeous.

Megan leaned forward to kiss the smile off her face. "Are you sure?"

Gianna pulled back just enough to whisper against her

lips. "Don't make me beg, Megan." She thrust her tongue briefly into Megan's mouth, then lay back again.

Tempted as Megan was to demand that Gianna beg, she felt chastened, scolded. She swallowed and reached for Gianna's mound again, though it wasn't the same. She still wanted to make her come, but... she wasn't sure she could.

She began rubbing at Gianna's clit again, staying around it and over the hood, being careful not to touch the sensitive tip. She felt that her motions were rote, mechanical, but either Gianna didn't notice the difference or she was determined to keep up the pretense for Megan's sake; she was panting and moaning again, pushing her hips up off the bed as though she wanted to get closer to Megan's fingers.

Megan knew exactly what she'd done wrong. She should never have assumed; she should have kept on asking, like she had at first, wanting to know every one of Gianna's weak points and pleasure spots. But Cari had always wanted all the feeling she could get, and she couldn't or wouldn't come unless Megan rubbed—or, her preference, licked—that most sensitive bundle of nerves.

She bit her lip as she watched Gianna, her black hair falling in damp strands across her faced as she moaned and writhed with pleasure. She was gorgeous, and Megan didn't feel like she could ever get enough. She wasn't Cari, and that was a good thing.

Gianna had spoken up, had explained what she wanted nicely, Megan reminded herself. She hadn't hit her or even shouted when she got it wrong. She was just the right way to wean off Cari.

She might have pressed harder with that thought, or maybe she'd just reached the peak, because Gianna finally screamed, arching her back and driving her elbows into the mattress. Megan could feel her throbbing under her touch, and she held her fingers there, keeping up a gentle pressure until Gianna finally gasped and collapsed limply onto the sheets.

Megan watched her for a moment, until her eyes fluttered open and she gestured weakly with one hand. "Come here."

Megan crawled closer, shifting herself up the bed, and Gianna put her arm around Megan's shoulder and pulled her close. They were both damp and sticky with sweat, but Megan felt no desire to get up.

Something thumped suddenly, a few rhythmic *whacks*, a pause, and then a few more. Megan couldn't tell whether it was coming from above or below, but she burst out laughing.

"What's so funny?" Gianna asked lazily.

"My neighbors," Megan said, her body shaking with the laughter, making Gianna's flesh jiggle as well. "I hoped they could hear us, and I guess they could. For once it's them pounding on the floor or the ceiling to make me shut up."

Gianna's grin curled up the corners of her mouth. "I take it they're usually the ones having noisy sex?"

"No, it's the screaming baby upstairs most of the time," Megan said. "And the dancers below. Living above dancers probably isn't as bad as living below them would be, but I don't really want to find out."

Gianna laughed and snuggled contentedly. "Then I guess we'll just have to give them more shows."

CHAPTER 7

Hey, Megan read in the text from Gianna. *Haven't heard from you for a few days. You're not ghosting on me, are you?*

Megan swallowed and put the phone back under her desk quickly. She didn't want anyone—specifically, Karen—to catch her texting at work, but she couldn't help reading her texts when she knew they came from Gianna. They'd been sending each other texts a few times a day since they'd slept together, but Megan hadn't seen Gianna in that time.

It wasn't that she didn't want to. It definitely wasn't that she hadn't been thinking about Gianna.

Maybe she was thinking about her too much. She didn't want this to get serious. The last time she'd gotten serious about a girl... well, that was Cari. She didn't think Gianna would blame her for hitting back, but she didn't want to find out, either.

But she couldn't bear to let Gianna think she was ignoring her, either. She considered and discarded several possible responses before deciding to go with the most sarcastic option.

You wish. I can't disappear—you know where I skate.

The response came back almost immediately. *That's right, I do. You can't get away from me.*

She didn't know how to respond to that, so she just put the phone back under her desk and pretended to do some work on her computer. She could have actually been doing work, except she couldn't concentrate on the words on the screen; her thoughts were all on Gianna's next text.

Thankfully, there was a call on the work phone a few minutes later, and work mode turned back on. She cheerily booked a couple for an hour's worth of trampoline time, successfully persuading the man on the other end to spring for extra to let him and his date into the black-light room. He believed her when she said that it would be romantic.

As soon as she hung up the phone, though, her thoughts returned to Gianna. What if the two of them used the trampolines as a date? They couldn't do that. There had been enough winks, nudges, and dirty jokes when Joe had learned that Megan was a lesbian. She did not want to endure the ribbing that would ensue when he met her hot date.

Besides, she wasn't sure they'd be able to keep their hands off each other, and that definitely wasn't allowed on the trampolines.

She checked her phone guiltily, but to her surprise,

there was another text from Gianna. She swiped it eagerly, realizing that she must have missed the buzz while she was on the phone.

So since I know where you skate and where you work, how about another date this Friday? I'll pick you up. I'm going to need some adult interaction after spending a week with these kids.

Before Megan could really start to wonder if she'd imagined the innuendo in Gianna's invitation, another text came through. This was just a row of winking emojis. She snorted with laughter and quickly shoved the phone back under the desk.

She wanted to respond to Gianna right away, saying yes, but she held herself back. Was this really what she wanted to do? So far, Gianna had been in control of every date—she'd asked Megan out, and she'd planned it and picked the spot.

Megan wanted to be in control. She wanted to be the one making decisions. But she was afraid that if she did that, she would be wrong. She didn't want to upset Gianna—not if it could be avoided.

She had been unable to avoid hitting Cari back that last day. That had been a collision course right from the beginning. And she could never have avoided Cari's fists, short of breaking up with her before things escalated that far; she understood that. But it was a hard habit to break.

She turned back to her work instead of making a decision. She could clear her mind while she made notes on the next month's schedule. Maybe her subconscious could work in the background.

A few minutes later, her phone buzzed again, and her heart leapt into her throat. Was Gianna upset that she hadn't responded again? Did she think Megan was really trying to ghost on her?

When she saw the name on the text, though, her beating heart turned into a cold lump. It was her older sister, Bonnie. Megan had idolized her sister as a kid, but as she'd gotten older, she'd realized that her sister's habit of picking on her one minute and beating up anybody else who said anything the next wasn't exactly healthy. They'd had a big fight around their parents' divorce and hadn't been close since. Besides, Bonnie hated roller derby.

U at work? Bonnie's text read.

Megan exhaled, typed a quick *Yes,* and set her phone aside. Hopefully that would be the end of it.

Unfortunately, her phone buzzed again. *Don't forget abt bachelor party for Dad.*

Megan rolled her eyes and didn't respond. She had no intention of going to their father's bachelor party. Not only was it creepy to invite your daughters to your bachelor party, she hadn't gotten along with her dad in a long time. In the divorce, Bonnie had sided with their dad and Megan had chosen their mom—who actually supported her by occasionally coming to a derby match.

Anyway, Megan had a derby match that night, just like

every Saturday. Shelly would tell her she could skip a game or two—the others did sometimes—but Megan didn't think she could be comfortable in herself if she went to a party instead of playing roller derby.

As though the thought had summoned her, yet another text vibrated Megan's phone, but this time it was from Shelly. Megan went for it eagerly. Finally, someone whose message she could read with no misgivings.

You're coming to my party Friday, right? it said. *Do you want a ride from work?*

Megan grinned. Now she knew what to say to Gianna, and she had something to look forward to, as well. How could she have forgotten that Shelly's birthday was on Friday?

I'll take the bus, she wrote. *I want to dress up properly for your party.*

OK, good, Shelly wrote back. *I can get home early and start cooking.*

Yeah, there was no way Megan was missing Shelly's party or her cooking. She wondered why Shelly had texted her instead of just mentioning it at practice tonight or Thursday night; was the whole team not invited? Now that she thought about it, she didn't remember Shelly mentioning the party in front of the whole team. She probably didn't want an entire roller derby team in her house, to be fair, but it gave Megan a warm feeling inside to know that she was one of the ones Shelly had chosen.

That did mean she definitely couldn't go out with Gianna on Friday night. But having plans put the control back in her hands.

This Friday is booked, she wrote back to Gianna at last. *How about next Friday? Pick me up at work and I'll tell you where to go.*

That sounds great, Gianna wrote back, almost too quickly. Like she'd been waiting with her phone by her hand. She was at work, wasn't she?

Megan turned back to her work with satisfaction. And if she was forcing Gianna to wonder whether she was going out with someone else this Friday, well...

Let her wonder.

People stared at Megan as she got on the bus near her house, and they stared again when she got off. She was happy to see it. She knew she stuck out a little bit with her bright hair and her septum piercing, even when she was dressed for work, but she only tolerated that. Now, done up in bright makeup and screaming clothes, she felt like she had her roller derby armor on—even if she wasn't in uniform right now.

She walked up to Shelly's door, gift tucked under her arm, and knocked, then pushed the door open. Shelly was facing the door with two people behind her—Gayle, and a pretty woman Megan didn't know. Shelly shrieked and ran toward Megan to sweep her up in a hug. "You came!"

"Did you think I was going to stand you up?" Megan asked, laughing and hugging her back. "Here—" She released Shelly and held out her wrapped gift.

"Oh, you didn't have to," Shelly said, but she looked delighted as she took the package. She opened it right away, shrieked in delight again at the book Megan had gotten her, and then pulled her over to the others.

"Megan, this is my good friend April," she said. Was that a wink? Megan was sure she was imagining things. "I think you two might get along."

"Nice to meet you," April said with a cherry-red smile. She and Megan shook hands.

"A few more girls from the team are coming, plus a few people you haven't met yet," Shelly said. "That includes my brother, who is going to be so thrilled at being surrounded by screaming girls."

Gayle snorted. "He'll be thrilled until he finds out we're all lesbians."

Shelly smiled, looking away from Gayle. "Yeah, that's kind of my point. But be nice to him, okay? He loves watching me play, but keeps making excuses when I ask him about refereeing or helping out in any way. I think getting into derby would do him some good."

"Oh, great," April said. "I'm not the only one here who isn't a derby girl, am I?"

"Don't worry," Shelly assured her, patting her on the shoulder. "Mia and a couple others from college are supposed to come. But you'll like the derby girls."

April grinned. "I'm sure I will."

Another knock came, and Shelly went to answer it, shrieking again when she opened it to Kristine and Mindy. She hugged them both. Gayle grunted, and Megan turned, giving her a questioning look.

"I was the first one here, and she didn't hug *me*," Gayle muttered, quiet enough that no one else could hear her under the sounds of Shelly welcoming Kristine and Mindy.

Megan frowned. "Maybe she was just surprised. She had to get her energy up to hug everyone."

Gayle shrugged. "Maybe."

She looked as unconvinced as Megan felt, though. Shelly was always very physically demonstrative, giving everyone hugs and kisses on the cheek or forehead. It was a good attitude in a team captain, even if it had freaked Megan out a little when she'd first joined the team—Cari had never liked it when someone else touched her, even Shelly.

So Shelly skipping a hug with Gayle was weird. Did she not like Gayle? If not, why had she been invited to the party?

"Okay, guys, there's drinks and chips out on the dining room table. Beers in the fridge. Megan, you want to come help me with the veggie tray?"

"Sure," Megan said, following her through the dining room and into the kitchen. Shelly ducked into the fridge and came out with a plastic-covered tray of crudités in one hand and two beers in the other. Megan took one of the beers and twisted off the cap.

"You didn't need any help with the veggies," she said as Shelly tore the plastic off the top and flicked some of the small pieces of broccoli and cauliflower back into their own compartments. There was a delicious smell emanating from the oven, but Shelly didn't seem to be in any hurry to open it.

Shelly grinned at her. "I just wanted to make sure you noticed April. She's recently single, too, and in need of some no-strings-attached fun just as much as you are, if not more so. She's hot, right?"

"Oh." Megan had noticed how pretty April was, but hadn't thought beyond that. No wonder Shelly had winked at her. "Yeah, she is."

She heard another knock at the door, and Shelly pushed the tray toward her. "Here, find a spot for this at the table." She rushed out of the room.

Megan took a swig of her beer before carrying the tray out. It had never occurred to her to look for a potential date at Shelly's party, even though she knew Shelly knew lots of queer girls. Of course, Shelly didn't know she was dating Gianna.

But she and Gianna didn't have any kind of exclusivity agreement. They weren't girlfriends. She could see where things went with April, couldn't she? From the way April had been grinning at her earlier, there was no lack of interest on that end.

She went back out to the table and pushed some of the

drinks aside to make space for the veggies, then took a carrot stick and crunched on it so she wouldn't have to talk to anyone.

Shelly's brother had arrived, and she was introducing him around. His name was David. His smile seemed to twitch upward when he was introduced to Megan, and she grinned back at him, almost laughing. Did he really not know that none of Shelly's friends were straight?

Shortly afterward, Tara arrived, and then two other girls who seemed to know April. They were the last of the guests.

Megan eyed the party. "You know, if we had skates, and decided to let the boy in, we could have a decent jam right now."

Shelly snorted. "Don't you ever think about anything other than roller derby?"

"Sure I do. When I'm at work, and can't play. You have some extra skates, don't you?"

"Yeah, but none that would fit David. And anyway, you're not skating on my floor."

"We could—"

"You're not tearing up my backyard, either. And anyway, it's too small." Shelly grinned at Megan's disappointment. "Maybe if we had ten girls, so I could persuade David to ref, I'd consider a little scrimmage. But not everyone plays. I invited Leya, but she gave some excuse."

Megan nodded. She wasn't surprised. None of them

knew Leya Out's real name—well, maybe Shelly did, but she was respecting Leya's privacy. She was a very good player, but she was quiet and didn't talk about herself. Megan would have liked to get to know her better, but she would never pry.

April was walking toward them, a drink in her hand. Shelly nudged Megan's arm. "Go talk to her."

Megan didn't have to go to her. April stopped right in front of her, smiling. She was curvy, but not as lush as Gianna; her asymmetrical bob didn't flatter her face. "So you're one of Shelly's roller derby friends, right?"

Megan nodded. "I'm a jammer. I—have you seen any games?"

April shook her head. "I'm usually busy on Saturday nights. Shelly has sworn to drag me to a game one of these days, though."

"Well, I try to get past the blockers—people like Gayle. Shelly usually plays blocker, too."

April nodded, her mouth twitching. "Yeah, I know how the game works. I've heard a lot about it."

"Oh." Megan didn't know what to say next. She'd thought explaining the game of roller derby to April would be a good conversation topic.

Or maybe she really just didn't know how to talk about anything other than derby.

No, that wasn't true. She talked with Gianna about all kinds of things—work, books, family. And she'd barely mentioned derby to Joe and Karen. The only times they cared about her after-work activities was when they were trying to persuade her to work late.

"So what do you do for a living?" April asked, as though she were reading Megan's mind—or as though she was fishing around for a conversation topic. Shelly had probably pushed her to talk to Megan, too.

"Oh, I work as a receptionist. At a trampoline park."

April's eyes lit up. "That's so cool! Do you get to bounce around after hours for free?"

Megan laughed. "No, I wish. My bosses would never stand for that. Anyway, it's open late and I only work during the day. I'd have to come back again to bounce after hours, and who wants to go back to work in the middle of the night?"

"I would if I worked in a trampoline park."

"What do you do?"

"Oh, I'm studying to be an architect."

Megan nodded and half-listened as April described her graduate school drama. April was quite attractive, and Megan enjoyed talking to her. Once they'd gotten over the initial awkwardness, conversation flowed easily. Megan thought she would enjoy hanging out with April for a long while.

But she didn't feel any spark like she did with Gianna. And she knew why. She wasn't arguing with April. There was no friction between them like with Gianna. It might not be healthy, but it seemed like that was what she craved in a relationship.

Was it a relationship with Gianna? It was some kind of relationship, that was for sure. But Megan didn't want to define it. She wasn't ready for another girlfriend, and "hate sex," while accurate, wasn't a complete picture of their relationship.

"What do you think?" April asked, blinking her long-lashed eyes at Megan, and Megan realized that she'd gotten so distracted that she had no idea what April's question was about.

"Uh, I don't really have an opinion," she hazarded. "I mostly think about roller derby."

April looked slightly puzzled, but didn't argue. However, she didn't continue the conversation, either.

Megan swigged her beer and realized that it was now empty. She needed another drink; maybe that would help her have an appropriate level of interest in April. After all, Shelly was probably right—she needed to go fast and loose for a while. She obviously wasn't psychologically over Cari, and someone she *didn't* have friction with would be healthy for her.

"Can I grab you another drink?" she asked April. "What were you drinking?"

April's mouth turned back up into a smile and she batted her eyelashes again. She did have pretty lips and lovely eyes. "Sure. I had a mojito. That girl over there is making drinks." She nodded toward the buffet table, where indeed, what looked like a full bar was laid out and Gayle was pouring things into a shaker.

Megan walked over just as Gayle was pouring out a bright pink drink and handing it over to one of April's friends. "You don't have to make drinks for everybody," she said.

"I like making drinks," Gayle said, and indeed, she was grinning, her cheeks a little flushed. "I asked Shelly if she minded, and she said that's why she got everything out. Can I make something for you?"

"Uh, I was going to get another mojito for April."

"Absolutely!" Gayle ducked under the buffet for a glass and picked some mint leaves off a plant on the windowsill to add to the bottom. "How are things going with her?"

"Okay, I guess. What, did Shelly put you on spying?"

"No, I just noticed the way she was looking at you. Which means things are going well, by the way."

"Huh." Megan looked around. Her eyes fell on Shelly first. She winked, but Megan wasn't sure she'd been looking at her. When she did find April, she was looking away.

"Here." Gayle handed the very pretty mojito over to Megan. "Can I make something for you?"

Megan smiled. "No, thanks. I'm just going to grab another beer."

"Oh, come on. There must be something you like as much as beer."

Megan's mind flashed back to that first date with

Gianna—the surprisingly rich wine, and then the taste of Gianna's lips, flushed with the dinner and drinks...

"No hard liquor you don't hate?"

Megan coughed, coming back to the present day. "Rum is okay."

"I'll make you a dark and stormy, how's that sound?"

"Good. I better eat something if you're going to be boozing me up, though."

"You better eat something anyway."

Megan watched as Gayle deftly poured ice from a scoop, not spilling a single chip. She really did seem to be enjoying herself. "Why aren't you a bartender if you like it so much?" She wasn't entirely sure she remembered what Gayle did for a living, but she was pretty sure it was some kind of office job—Megan would have remembered if Gayle was a bartender.

Gayle shook her head. "I hate people."

Megan snorted. "That explains the roller derby. Aren't people easier if you get them drunk?"

"No, they're so much worse. I bartended for a while in college, but I couldn't stand the people. I mean, you know, right? You're a receptionist or something. You probably need roller derby every day just to deal with the customers."

"No, I love the customers. They're the best part of the job."

"Really?" Gayle stared at her for a moment, then held out her drink. "I don't get you, Splatwood, but I like you anyway."

Megan took the drink and grinned. "Cheers, Blocksalot." She took a sip of her drink. "This is good."

"Thank you. Eat something."

Megan obediently walked toward the table, set down her drink, and started shoving chips into her face. It wasn't until she absentmindedly lifted her glass to her face, had her nose tickled by the mint garnish, and discovered that she was about to drink the wrong thing, that she remembered she'd originally walked over to Gayle in order to get a drink for April.

She looked around for April and found her chatting with Shelly, but her arms were crossed. *Shit. Lost that chance for sure.*

But she didn't feel bad about it. In fact, other than the guilt over literally forgetting about April, she felt all right. She grabbed a few veggies and walked over to April and Shelly.

"Here's your mojito," she said, holding it out. "I'm sorry—I was an idiot just now." As soon as April took the drink, Megan shoved a piece of broccoli into her mouth so she wouldn't be tempted to talk more and explain herself.

"Yeah, thanks," April said, sipping the mojito and then turning away. Her two friends were in the living room, and she went to join them.

Shelly raised her eyebrows at Megan. "What was that about? I thought you'd like her."

Megan shook her head and shrugged, trying to

communicate her innocence while still chewing her broccoli. When she had swallowed, she said, "I do like her, but not enough, I guess. I didn't mean to ditch her. I just totally forgot I was talking to her."

"You call that liking someone?"

Megan shrugged again, helplessly. "I can't explain my brain, Shell. You put me on skates or behind a reception desk and I'm great. Otherwise, I don't know how to deal with people."

"You seemed to deal with Mountain Bruise just fine a couple of weeks ago."

Megan looked down at her drink, her stomach twisting with anxiety. "That was... different. We barely talked. Anyway, she started it."

"The way you are on the track, I'm surprised you let anyone else start anything."

Megan swallowed, not knowing what to say. She didn't know how to explain to Shelly that she was a different person on the track and off it. Shelly herself seemed to be the same either way, but Megan knew she wasn't the only one with this split—Leya was practically silent off the track, but she was just as aggressive as any of them on it.

She darted her eyes around the room, seeking a topic to change the conversation to, and spied Gayle holding up a glass as she carefully poured liquor into it. "You seem to have found the right way to keep Gayle entertained."

Shelly immediately turned to Gayle, her eyes lighting

up and a smile tugging at her lips. "She does seem to be having a good time, doesn't she? I'm glad I thought to put together a full bar."

"Not your usual setup?" Megan watched Shelly curiously. She hadn't thought changing the subject would go over well at all, but Shelly seemed to be enthralled.

"No, you know me, I'd normally be fine with a couple of six-packs. Maybe more for a party this size. But I think you're the only one who's even had a beer."

"Yeah, Gayle wouldn't let me get away without making me a fancy drink."

"Oh, you're going to blame her for letting April down?"

And there it was. Shelly had turned toward her again and was smirking. "Go tell her about how awkward you are. Maybe you can salvage it."

Megan shook her head firmly. "I blew it with April and I'm okay with that. I don't need anything from her. If we start talking naturally again, that's fine." She heard a snippet of conversation—Tara was talking to someone about derby. That was a conversation she wanted to join in.

As she turned, she said to Shelly, "If you have any more hot friends you want to introduce me to, I'm all for it."

But somehow she didn't think she would be.

CHAPTER 8

A week—and a lot of roller derby—gave Megan enough time to mull over how she felt about April and where she was going to take Gianna for their date.

She decided that there were two things at play with April. One, she obviously was way more into a girl she could fight with. If Gianna hadn't been around, she would have been more interested in April, but her libido was disappointed at the lack of tension. Two, even though consciously she knew that she didn't have any kind of exclusivity with Gianna, her subconscious wasn't convinced. She'd never really dated casually before; when she was in college she'd pursued one girl at a time until she got rejected, and when she started dating Cari they were joined at the hip. Megan was more wired to be a serial monogamist, and that was fine with her.

The only question that remained was whether she

should talk to Gianna about exclusivity. She hadn't been able to decide, and figured they would talk about it if it came up. She didn't know if Gianna had been dating other girls, and didn't really want to know. Mostly because Gianna had said she was a slut and if she *was* sleeping with anyone else, Megan did not want confirmation.

The date was the easy part. She knew Gianna well enough now to know where they could go that they would both enjoy. A certain museum was close to Megan's heart, and to her dark sense of humor, which Gianna had made it clear she appreciated.

Accordingly, that morning she picked out a dress printed with skulls, roses, and—not obviously distinct from the roses until you looked closely—anatomical hearts. Pulling it out of her closet and holding it up gave her an unexpected blow; she'd bought the dress after a fight with Cari and hadn't worn it since the breakup. For a moment she wondered if she should throw it away.

But she loved the subtle goriness of the print, and she thought Gianna would like it, too. Besides, it was perfect for the Mütter Museum. So she wore it, with a red cardigan over it so her bosses and the customers wouldn't be able to look too closely at the print.

The day flew by—probably because she was nervous—and Gianna arrived to pick her up right on time. This time the parking lot was crowded, since there was a party that evening, but Megan picked out Gianna's little red convertible immediately and hurried her steps to meet it.

"So where are we going?" Gianna asked when Megan got in, folding her cardigan over her lap.

Megan didn't answer immediately; she was distracted by the scarlet dress Gianna was wearing, the satiny fabric hugging every curve. "Uh, you didn't have to dress up."

Gianna grinned. "Would you believe this is just what I wore to work today?"

"Absolutely not. You'd give the parents heart attacks."

"I like to shock. But no, I just dressed up for you. Come on, am I going north or south?"

Megan swallowed. She wondered if she should change her mind, take Gianna somewhere more appropriate for that dress. But she didn't know where they could go that would be fancy enough for Gianna's dress (the opera?) and yet where her own dress wouldn't look out of place.

"Uh, south. And west."

"Got it." Gianna whipped the car out of the parking lot, her usual reckless driving style. If Megan hadn't seen her playing with the little girl at the afterparty, she would never be able to believe that Gianna was a kindergarten teacher.

"What do you usually wear to work?" she asked.

"Oh, you'd never recognize me. I'm usually in jeans and a long-sleeved T-shirt that covers everything, and I wear my hair up."

"I think I'd recognize you," Megan said with a grin. "You'd have cleavage even in a turtleneck."

"Are you saying you recognize my cleavage, not my face?"

"Face? You have a face?"

Gianna snorted. "I suppose I should have seen that coming."

Megan directed her to a parking garage, then led the way to the Mütter Museum. Gianna gasped as they approached it. "Are we going to the Mütter? Oh, wow, I've always wanted to go there, but haven't had the time."

"Really? You've never been?"

Gianna clutched Megan's arm. "I can't justify this to the school board as an appropriate kindergarten field trip. I go to the Franklin Institute two or three times a year, but never here. Oh, I can't wait!"

Megan found an extra bounce in her step as she led the way into the museum. Clearly, changing their destination just to match Gianna's dress would have been a mistake.

"Oh my god, I *love* your dress," the woman at the front desk said as she accepted Megan's cash. She had dyed blue hair and stretched earlobes. Her eyes roamed up and down over Megan's body.

Megan blushed. "Thanks. I thought it suited the occasion."

The woman gave her a cute grin, her front teeth peeking out over her lower lip. Then Gianna reached out and grabbed Megan's hand. The woman's smile immediately faded.

"Here you go," she said, holding out the change and the tickets. "You two have a great time. Don't miss the Soap Lady."

“The soap lady?” Gianna asked in an undertone. “Oh, and by the way, that is a nice dress.”

“Thanks,” Megan said, rolling her eyes. “So kind of you to notice. And we’ll get to the Soap Lady. I want to take you around to everything in order.”

Gianna gasped as they entered the main exhibit hall. “Is that really a wall of skulls?”

Megan had been to the museum a few times before, so she enjoyed Gianna’s reactions at least as much, if not more, than the actual museum exhibits. And when Gianna laughed, her whole body jiggled in that slinky red dress.

It was interesting that Megan was still attracted to her when they weren’t fighting. But she wasn’t going to complain.

Gianna was entertained by the skulls, the primitive forceps, and the book bound in human skin, but a little more grossed out by the Soap Lady, whose corpse had turned into a waxy substance after death, and some of the things in jars. Megan loved it all, but she didn’t mind that Gianna wasn’t one hundred percent enthusiastic.

Especially when Gianna pulled her into a bathroom, pressed her up against a wall, and started whispering in her ear while her hand roamed over Megan’s body. If a museum worker hadn’t walked in a moment later, she didn’t know how far that would have gone.

Finally, though, they finished their tour of the museum, and strolled out into a cool evening. Megan shivered, wishing she hadn’t left her cardigan in the car. Gianna stretched her arms into the air and said, "I'm starving. Did you have a plan for dinner?"

"I hadn't thought about it," Megan admitted. "The museum was as far as I got in planning."

Gianna grinned at her. "Well, it was a good plan. How about we go back to my place and order takeout? I think I've had enough of being out in public."

Megan's heart leapt. "Yeah, that sounds great." She'd wanted to see Gianna's home, but had hesitated to push too hard for it.

It turned out that Gianna lived in a tall, beautiful apartment building in West Philly, high enough to be worth taking the elevator to. Unfortunately, since it was surrounded by other tall buildings, she didn't have a view to match the height, but the apartment was a lot nicer than Megan's.

"What do you like?" Gianna asked, pulling a stack of menus off the fridge. "I have Chinese, Indian, Thai, Ethiopian, and we could find something else online."

"Whatever you want," Megan said, looking around. She was being nosy, but she didn't really care. Anyway, she'd seen Gianna naked; what more could her apartment reveal?

She walked over to the couch, which had a stack of parenting magazines on one of the cushions and faced a darkwood coffee table and a large TV. "Your place is really nice."

"It's too big for me," she said. "But my parents insisted I get a good place. They paid the deposit for me. Here, pick something. I'll order." She handed Megan the Thai menu.

Megan took it, but pointed at the parenting magazines

before she looked at the menu. "What are those for, research?"

"Hmm?" Gianna leaned over the back of the couch and laughed. "They usually have a lot of craft ideas, sometimes other things that I can use for the kids. And when I'm done with them, they're great for collages. Let me get rid of those so we can use the couch."

"Are you sure they're not for teasing your parents? My mom would be thrilled if she thought I was going to have kids."

"Nope. I love my parents, and taunting them that way would be cruel." Gianna walked around Megan, giving her a jolt as their skin brushed together. But Gianna didn't seem to notice; she bent over the arm of the couch and gathered up the magazines. Megan quickly turned to the menu and picked out something to eat.

She looked around the apartment some more as Gianna placed the call. It had two bedrooms, one of which contained a bed; the other had a sewing machine and a number of bins stacked around.

"You sew?" she asked once Gianna was off the phone.

"Yeah, some. I put together outfits for derby. I used to sew my own clothes more, but there isn't as much time now." She walked over to the doorway of the sewing room, pressing her hip against Megan's side. "You seem like you'd be crafty."

Megan laughed and shook her head. "They tried to teach me to knit and sew in middle school. They failed. The only things I'm good at are roller skating and selling people on the trampoline park."

"Oh," Gianna said, "I think you're good at a few more things."

And then they were kissing, Megan's back pressed against the doorjamb, Gianna's curves pressed to her front. Megan was warm again, but she couldn't get her cardigan off; there was no room between their bodies for her hands. Instead she let her hand slide over Gianna's back, the dip in for her waist, and then the flare of her hips and ass. The silky fabric of Gianna's dress made it easy.

Gianna's hands were roaming over her body, too, sliding over her thighs, down to her knees, and then she was bunching up Megan's dress and sliding her hands underneath. Megan had time for the hazy thought that Gianna's enthusiasm was very sudden before those clever little hands had found her panties and dipped underneath them.

She made a surprised cry into Gianna's mouth, and that gave Gianna the opening to thrust her tongue inside, at the same moment as she pushed two fingers into Megan's opening. Megan clutched Gianna's ass with both hands, feeling as though she was falling, as though she needed Gianna to hold her up.

Gianna's fingers were inside her, and her tongue, and her free hand was squeezing Megan's breasts, pressing them one at a time until her nipples stood up hard and sweat dripped down her spine. She was squirming, writhing against Gianna's touch, wanting more.

Gianna's thumb found her clit, and Megan pushed her hips forward, wanting more pressure, more touch. Gianna obliged, rubbing hard and fast until Megan was coming, pleasure exploding through every nerve, her body going rigid for a moment before every muscle seemed to melt and she really did have to hang on to Gianna to hold herself up.

The phone rang. "Oh, damn," Gianna said, detaching herself from Megan. "That will be the food. I really need it now."

Megan held onto the doorway until she could walk again.

A week later, Monstrous Regiment was playing Rolling in the Streets again, and Megan could see the difference in Gianna's playing. It wasn't that she had any more or less energy—in fact, Megan couldn't really define what it was. Gianna just seemed sharper, more jagged, somehow.

She didn't know whether being around the kindergarteners all day wore Gianna out or just gave her something to work off at roller derby. Maybe it was both—Megan could certainly empathize with that. Sometimes Joe and Karen felt like kindergarteners.

She supposed she would find out, both about the kindergarteners and about Gianna, in just under two weeks when they all came to the trampoline park.

The first several jams of the match, she and Gianna weren't both on the track at the same time. Megan racked up the points; Monstrous Regiment was maintaining a slight lead, but it was still a lead, and she didn't let it slip at all.

But in her third jam, the last one before the halftime break, she and Gianna were both on the track. Gianna shot her a grin as she settled her helmet on her head. Megan grinned back, popping in her mouth guard to show she meant business. She was not going to let Gianna distract her this time.

And she didn't. All right, Gianna's tits bouncing under her uniform might have distracted her a *little* bit, but she still made lead jammer and started passing again before Kiss With a Fist had made it all the way through.

Rolling in the Streets seemed to be more energetic this time; maybe their last game against Monstrous Regiment had pumped them up, or maybe something else had happened in the weeks in between. They might have had more wins, but Monstrous Regiment hadn't lost a game since the win that Rolling in the Streets had barely scraped up.

Megan pushed and wiggled her way through the blockers, careful not to use her elbows, even when she was really, really tempted to. Britney Scares almost knocked her over, but Gayle got in Britney's way and Megan spun past them both.

She was past the blockers—four points to her team. But that was only four. Where was Gianna?

Mountain Bruise seemed to come out of nowhere, flying at Megan and knocking her backward. Megan toppled over, laughing, both because of how ridiculous she felt and because she had, once again, been knocked over by Gianna's delicious ass.

She landed on her back, getting the wind knocked out of her, but she barely had time to react to that before something hit her shoulder even harder. She screamed, half in surprise, half in pain. For a moment she saw stars.

A whistle blew and then there was a crowd around her. "I'm all right," she gasped, reaching for Shelly's hand to help herself up.

But she couldn't get up. Her shoulder screamed at her, and Gianna was leaning over her. "Oh shit, oh shit, I'm sorry! Did I break anything?"

"What?" Megan didn't understand what was going on. "My shoulder..."

She couldn't have her first roller-derby injury. It was too ridiculous. She hadn't hurt herself by hitting the floor or the wall, or even by tripping over someone or something—someone had skated *into* her?

"I'll get her to the emergency room," Shelly was saying. "That looks like it could be broken."

"No, I'll take her." Gianna's voice was shaking. "Janine, would you get me my shoes? I'm the one that hit her, I should be out of the match anyway. And this way we're down one person on each team. It's still a fair game."

"No, no, we should end the game," Shelly said. "Call it a draw."

"Don't you fucking dare," Megan said. She swallowed,

trying to get up again, and this time—using her uninjured right arm—she pushed herself to a sitting position. "Call this jam but don't call the game. Win it for me, Shelly."

Shelly crouched down next to her, her mouth drawn with concern. "Are you sure? It's okay with you if Mountain Bruise drives you to the hospital?"

Megan nodded quickly. Right now, there were only a few people she wanted around her. Shelly would be great, but Gianna was even better. And she really didn't want the game to end. Her injury wasn't the end of the world; they had to win another game and reclaim their record from Rolling in the Streets.

Anyway, Gianna was already putting on her sneakers. She was right—it was more fair if both sides were down a single player.

Gayle was behind Shelly. She touched her shoulder, and Shelly looked up, startled. "We'll win for you, Megan. And I think she's going to be okay, Shell. She's been able to move the arm, so I don't think it's broken."

Megan nodded again. "Hurts like a bitch, though."

"Okay." Shelly reached for Megan, hesitated, and patted her right arm gingerly. "Some of us will come and see you after the game."

"After you win," Megan said, and managed a small smile.

Tara ran out onto the track just behind Gianna; she was towering (like her namesake) over the other player, even in her sock feet. "Let me help you get out to her car. Is that okay?"

"I can walk," Megan protested, but she was glad of Tara's help to get off the ground. With the pain she was in, she was none too steady on her skates. Tara sat her down, and she and Mindy took Megan's skates off and replaced them with her shoes. Shelly and Kiss With a Fist were talking to the referee now. It looked like the match would be starting up again once she and Gianna were out of there.

Tara walked her to Gianna's car and helped her buckle in, then waved and dashed back inside. "You going to be all right?" Gianna asked, glancing over at Megan as she started up the car.

"Yes," Megan said, gritting her teeth against the acceleration as Gianna tore out of the parking lot. "It's probably not broken. But damn, I hope they don't tell me I have to stop playing roller derby."

Gianna laughed, but it didn't sound happy.

Megan stared out the window at the lights they sped past, her stomach churning. What if they did tell her she had to stop? Most derby injuries did mean you had to take a break, at least. She didn't know what she would do with her time. She didn't know what she would do with her *life*.

Thankfully, she didn't have to wallow for long. The way Gianna drove, her shoulder screamed at every turn and every stoplight, but at least she got them quickly to the hospital.

Megan checked in at the emergency-room desk, then turned to see that Gianna had found them seats together. She sat down with a groan. The waiting room was crowded, and she suspected her injury was just bad enough to make waiting agony, without being bad enough to make it short. She considered going back to the desk and asking for a painkiller, but she had a suspicion that asking would be a good way to not get any.

"Want me to go find a bookstore while you wait?" Gianna said. "Or it might be faster just to drive home and find something for you to read."

Megan let out a sigh. "No, thanks. I don't think I'd be able to concentrate, and anyway, I'd rather have you here."

It was strange to realize just how much she meant it. She didn't like hospitals—they didn't freak her out or anything, she just didn't enjoy the smell, the bustle, or the knowledge that some stranger had to take care of her. She felt better having Gianna there, a buffer against the world.

So her buffer was also the reason she was here. That was fine with her.

Gianna gave her a sideways grin. "That was a pretty spectacular fall, though."

Megan started to laugh, then stopped abruptly, hissing in a breath. Jiggling her shoulder was not fun. "Yeah, it would've been a great block if you hadn't skated right into me."

"I guess I need to work on my aim."

"Just hit people with your soft parts, not with your skates, and it should be fine."

"You like being hit with my soft parts."

Megan smirked. "Who wouldn't like it?"

"Straight girls, I guess."

"I think your soft parts are enough to make even straight girls really happy. And stop making me laugh, it hurts."

"Come on, suck it up. Are you a derby girl or aren't you?"

Megan was really struggling not to laugh now. "I didn't know you were a sadist. You really shouldn't spring that on me."

It didn't seem to take nearly as long as she feared before someone was calling her name and escorting her back to a room, though as she glanced behind her at the waiting room (to assure herself that Gianna was following, which she was), she realized that its entire population had changed.

They gave her a room with one other person in it, not a room alone, but that was all right; the other bed had a little old lady in it with another little old lady sitting beside her, and anyway, the bed was surprisingly comfortable. Megan sighed as she lay down.

"Let me take a look at that shoulder," the nurse, an East Asian woman who looked the same age as Megan, said, taking Megan by the wrist as she did and lifting her arm in the air. Megan hissed as she manipulated the shoulder.

"Not broken," the nurse said, picking up a clipboard and writing something down. "I'm guessing shoulder separation. We'll do an X-ray to see how bad it is."

Megan grimaced. "A shoulder separation sounds pretty bad."

The nurse shook her head. "It usually heals up on its

own. We'll get you into the X-ray room and then have the doctor take a look. She'll tell you how bad it is." Her voice was too tired to be reassuring.

"Can I get any painkillers?" Megan asked.

"Can you swallow pills?" The nurse didn't look up at her.

"Yes."

"We'll get you something." She'd probably had a long shift.

"Thanks." Megan swallowed the urge to say anything else to the nurse. She needed to get on with her night.

The nurse pulled the curtain between the beds as she left, and Gianna immediately took Megan's right hand. "Okay, that doesn't sound too bad."

"Except for the X-ray. Damn, I hope all this is covered under my insurance." It probably wasn't. Getting Joe and Karen to set up insurance for the small company had been bad enough; the insurance they had wasn't any better than what Megan could find on the marketplace.

Gianna squeezed her hand. "Hey, before you know it you'll be up and about better than ever." She stood up and planted a kiss on Megan's lips. Her breasts pressed against Megan's chest, jostling her injured shoulder, but desire still shot through Megan like she hoped the painkiller would soon.

She had to catch her breath when Gianna sat back down. "This is ridiculous. You broke my damn shoulder and I still want you."

Gianna grinned at her. "You heard the nurse. I didn't break anything. I just separated it."

Megan rolled her eyes. The bed was starting to feel uncomfortable, and it was hard to concentrate on their banter. "Yeah, first you separate my shoulder from my neck, then you'll separate me from my money. Is that how it goes?"

She thought her gold-digger joke was pretty feeble, but Gianna rolled with it. "You don't need to worry about that, babe. I'll take good care of you, forever and ever. You do look pretty cute all helpless on the bed like that."

Megan froze as panic crashed through her, all her muscles tensing up, the shoulder sending a jolt of pain through her body. "Don't say that." Her voice came out strained and harsh.

Gianna's eyes widened and her grin dropped off. "What? I'm sorry, babe. What did I say?"

"Don't act like... you want me powerless." Megan was in control this time. That was the only reason this relationship was okay. If she didn't have any power, any control, then Gianna was no better than Cari and she was better off alone.

Gianna swallowed and shook her head. "I didn't mean that. I was joking. I mean, you were joking about thinking I was going to take all your money, right? If you've been serious about everything you've said to me, I need to rethink this relationship." She grinned again, but it was weaker.

Megan nodded carefully. "You're right. I was joking. I'm sorry, I overreacted." Adrenaline still seemed to be pounding through her veins, but rationally, she knew she was telling the truth.

Gianna patted her uninjured shoulder. "It's okay, babe. If that's something that gets under your skin, I'll avoid it in the future."

Megan sighed. "Thanks."

Another nurse, a heavyset black woman with a warm smile, came in with two cups. "Here you go, miss, a pain-killer for you. And then I'll be back in a few minutes to take you to the X-ray room, all right? Give the painkiller a little time to work."

"Thank you," Megan said. Gianna helped her get the pill into her mouth, then she swallowed the cup of water, washing it down her throat.

The nurse turned to Gianna. "You her girlfriend?"

Well, that was a question Megan hadn't expected to hear. Her only comfort was that, based on Gianna's flushing cheeks and widening eyes, the same confusion was flooding her system as Megan's. "Uh..."

The nurse smirked. "Well, don't all answer at once. You can come to the X-ray room with us, if you're staying with her, but if you're planning to call anyone else you ought to do it now."

"I'll stay with her," Gianna said quickly.

"Good girl." The nurse gave a sharp nod and walked away.

She left silence behind her. Gianna and Megan stared

at each other, so quiet that Megan could pick out, over the hum of hospital equipment, the soft, almost papery whispers of the old women at the other bed. She hoped they were both a little deaf and hadn't been able to hear her conversation with Gianna.

"We don't have to talk about that now," Gianna said. "If you don't want to."

Megan swallowed. "Better now than once the painkiller hits my system." She had been thinking that if it came up, they would talk about it. But now she wasn't so sure she wanted to.

Gianna's hands were folded in her lap. "Look, I know I told you I was a slut, but I really like you, Megan, and I haven't seen anyone else since we met. It seems like you might have some, well, issues, so I didn't want to push it, but I'm ready to say this is a relationship if you are. If you're not, that's okay, too."

Megan stared at the ceiling and swore softly. "Are my issues really that obvious?"

"Only if you're paying attention," Gianna said.

"I guess that explains why you and Shelly are the only ones who've said anything." Megan took a deep breath, trying to order her thoughts. She liked Gianna a lot. She still liked her even now, when she was waiting in the hospital to have her injury tended after Gianna had knocked her down and skated into her shoulder. But was she ready to say she was her girlfriend?

She's nothing like Cari, an angry, insidious voice whispered inside her. But that would be a good thing. Also, it wasn't true.

They were definitely different people, but both Gianna and Cari had that strong presence, that power about them. It was a huge amount of confidence and plenty of sex appeal. It was also a great capacity for violence.

"I have a question," Megan said. She was still staring at the ceiling, not looking at Gianna. She hadn't thought of this until now... but now that she had, she wouldn't be able to stop worrying about it until she knew.

She would always hit back.

"I hope I can answer it."

"This is going to sound stupid. But you didn't do it on purpose, did you?"

"What? No, of course not. I mean, I blocked you on purpose, obviously. But I didn't expect to knock you over, and skating into you was a total accident. If you'd fallen at a different angle, I would have skated around you. Or possibly hit you in the head, and then we'd be having an entirely different conversation."

Megan turned her head to look at Gianna. "You weren't mad or anything?"

"No, absolutely not." Gianna held her gaze, hands stilled in her lap. "It was just roller derby, babe. I might go a little harder on you than I do on anyone else, but that's just because it's a lot more fun to crash into you than anyone else."

Megan smiled. "Thanks."

“Why would I be mad at you, anyway?”

“I don’t know.” She couldn’t think of anything. With Cari, she always would have been able to come up with something. So that was a good sign.

But the idea of declaring anything, of saying Gianna was her girlfriend, still made her stomach twist into knots. She shook her head. “I’m sorry. I’m not ready... Let’s just call it casually dating for now.”

“Okay,” Gianna said, too quickly.

“But for what it’s worth, I haven’t seen anyone else since we met, either.”

“Thank you,” she whispered.

CHAPTER 9

Gianna stayed with Megan while they took her to another room to be X-rayed, and while they took her back, and while she waited. They put her in a wheelchair to transport her; she didn't like it very much, and it was harder on her shoulder than walking would have been, but they insisted.

And she was, after all, a bit wobbly getting out of the wheelchair and back into her hospital bed. Must be the painkiller. It was working—she only had a little pain now.

They waited quietly for the results after the X-ray; neither of them could think of anything to say to break the silence. Gianna was still holding her hands clasped tightly together in her lap. Was she really that worried?

Finally, the doctor came in. She was bright-eyed and smiling; she must have gotten sleep more recently than the first nurse. "Megan? Good news. Nothing's broken."

"I thought so," Megan said, but she still felt relieved. "The nurse thought it was a shoulder separation."

The doctor nodded, still smiling. "It's not a bad one—no deformity, and as long as you let it heal on its own, there shouldn't be any. You're going to get a sling and I recommend that you keep the arm immobilized as much as possible. You should also be icing it. Come back in a week and we'll see how it's healing up, but I'm hoping after two weeks, if you treat it right, you'll be able to move normally again."

Megan swallowed. Two weeks? That meant missing at least one game—it felt like a lifetime. "Can I still play roller derby?"

That dropped the smile from the doctor's face. She looked confused. "That's on skates?"

"Yes. It's a full-contact sport. It's how I injured my shoulder."

Gianna, still silent, did not volunteer that the injury had come from her.

The doctor shook her head. "I have to recommend against it, at least for the first week until we see how it's healing up, but probably for longer. Even if you don't fall, you'll need to move your arms to keep your balance on skates, and like I said, you'll need to keep that arm immobilized. Do you have someone who can help you get dressed?"

Megan coughed in embarrassment. She hadn't been expecting that question. Gianna was looking away, but Megan was pretty sure she saw a blush. "Uh, no. Not really."

"You can move your arm a little when getting dressed,

but limit it. Try to choose clothes you can get on and off one-handed."

"Okay." No more cute dresses for a while.

"Do you need a note for your job?"

"No, I don't think so. I can still type and answer the phone, just maybe not both at once."

The doctor smiled. "I'll write you one just in case. Oh, here's your sling." The heavyset nurse from before came in carrying what looked like just a bundle of fabric. She smiled at Megan, who managed a smile back.

Between them, the nurse and the doctor got the sling onto Megan's arm and instructed her on its use. They also gave her a pamphlet (which was a relief, since she didn't think she could remember the instructions) and a prescription for more painkillers. Getting the sling on hurt, but once her arm was held in place, she felt fine.

Finally, they gave her some paperwork, took her to another waiting area, and told her to fill it out and who to take it to. She sighed as she sat down at a table, counting her blessings—at least it wasn't her right arm that was injured, and she could still write.

Gianna sat down across from her. "Megan?"

She jumped a little in the middle of writing her name, so that the X in her last name trailed down past the line. She finished it quickly and looked up. "Yeah?"

"Sorry to bug you in the middle of your paperwork, but while we're still alone, there's something I have to ask you."

Gianna still looked nervous, her hands hidden under the table but her arms not moving.

Megan sat up straighter, putting down the pen. She didn't want to make Gianna think she wasn't listening, though her stomach twisted with anxiety and most of her brain was telling her not to let Gianna ask the question. "Sure. Go ahead."

"I should have asked earlier. I was too nervous then, but I haven't been able to stop thinking about it."

This must be bad. She's stalling. Megan could have made a joke out of it, but instead she nodded, trying to tell Gianna to get on with it.

"The question you asked me earlier. About whether I hurt you on purpose. You said there wasn't any reason to think I was mad at you, but why else would you ask the question? What did I do that made you even think to ask that?"

Oh. That wasn't so bad. Megan took a deep breath. "It's not you. The question really wasn't about you at all. My ex..."

She swallowed, her throat suddenly dry. Sweat was breaking out on her forehead, and she lifted her left arm, only to be reminded by a twinge of pain that she shouldn't be moving it. She wiped her forehead with the derby wristband on her right arm instead.

She'd never talked to anyone about this. Not her parents, not her sister, not her friends in roller derby. She knew, intellectually, that she shouldn't be ashamed of it. That it wasn't really her fault her girlfriend hit her. But she was the one who'd never left—who hadn't even tried to leave. She was the one letting herself be tortured.

And in the end, like she'd always known, it had to be her who hit back.

"This is harder to talk about than I thought it would be," she confessed.

Gianna put her arm on her table, her hand close to Megan, lying palm up. After a moment, Megan took it. Gianna said nothing; Megan suspected that she wanted to be reassuring, but couldn't think of anything to say.

"Well, I can say that she wouldn't have done it like that," Megan said at last. "She was straightforward. She wouldn't have made it look like an accident." It was hard to speak, and she could hear her voice getting hoarser. "But she always said it was my fault."

"She hit you," Gianna said.

Megan nodded, ashamed that she couldn't say it herself.

"I'm not her," Gianna said.

"I know." She could speak again. This was easier to say. "But I had to make sure. I didn't want to be making the same mistake again, you know?"

Gianna took a deep breath and let it out slowly. "That makes sense. It's a smart thing to make sure of. But you don't still think you're making that mistake, do you? You didn't believe me?"

"I did believe you," Megan said. "I do."

But she wasn't sure if Gianna heard her. She was

raising her voice to be heard above the sudden shouts of "There she is!", but she didn't think it worked, and Gianna was turning toward the commotion.

At the other end of the room, Shelly, Gayle, Tara, Kristine, and Mindy were rushing in, still wearing their derby outfits, screaming and cheering. Megan felt her face stretch into a grin as she saw them. They could have had better timing, but at least they were saving her from the rest of this very uncomfortable conversation.

She stood up to greet them. "Careful," she said as she hugged them all one-handed. "I'm supposed to keep my shoulder immobilized."

"It's not broken, is it?" Kristine asked, her face pinched with anxiety. "How soon can you get back to derby?"

"It's not broken, just a shoulder separation," Megan said. "I can skate, but I can't—"

"That's not what the doctor said," Gianna interrupted her, throwing her arm out as though to physically stop Megan from talking.

Megan shook her head. "I just have to keep my arm immobilized."

"And you need to move your arms to keep your balance when you skate."

Megan rolled her eyes. "I'm not that amateur of a skater. I can skate at a reasonable speed without flailing my arms around."

"If the doctor said you shouldn't skate, you're not skating," Shelly said.

"She didn't say that."

"She didn't have to," Gianna said. She was standing now, too, her elbows pointed out with hands firmly planted on her hips. "She recommended against it. I'm not going to let you screw up your healing by messing with doctor's orders."

"And neither are we," Tara said firmly. "Thanks for watching out for her."

"She's right," Mindy said. "The better you follow doctor's orders, the sooner you'll be on the track again. We can't lose our star jammer for longer than absolutely necessary."

Megan scowled at Gianna. She wanted to cross her arms, but she couldn't, as a twinge of pain in her shoulder reminded her. She felt like Gianna had ripped something away from her, but in front of half her team, she couldn't exactly let loose.

Instead she swallowed, turned to Shelly, and said, "So you guys won, right?"

"Barely," Shelly said with a grin. "Two points up. Try not to get injured again, huh? We could have used you."

Megan managed to stretch her face into the semblance of a smile. "Right."

"We brought your bag with the rest of your stuff," Gayle said, lifting it to show her.

"Thanks. But I have to fill out this paperwork before I can leave."

"I'll drive you home," Shelly said immediately. "Everyone else can go. Or head to the afterparty, if you want."

"Megan, don't you want me to drive you home?" Gianna asked. Her hands were clasped in front of her again.

"It's fine," Shelly said. "I know where she lives. I've driven her there enough times."

Megan felt a sudden flutter of panic that Gianna would think she'd lied, that she'd been sleeping with Shelly. Then remembered it didn't matter what Gianna thought. She had never said that she'd been celibate between breaking up with Cari and meeting Gianna.

Besides, the way Gianna had interrupted her about the doctor, taking control away from her, made her nervous. Maybe there was a reason she wasn't able to agree to be Gianna's girlfriend.

"Shelly can take me home," she said. She smiled at Gianna. "Besides, you drive the same way you skate. I don't know if I'm safe in the car with you."

"Oh, that was mean," Mindy said with a giggle.

Gianna didn't smile. Megan's stomach twisted. "It was a joke," she said. "But really, you can go home. Thanks for taking me to the hospital. I'm just going to finish this paperwork." She sat down.

"Yeah, okay," Gianna said. She squeezed her hands together, then gave a quick, jerky gesture, like flicking water off her fingers. "I'll see you later, then."

She turned and walked away. Megan looked down at her paperwork and wrote her date of birth; she wouldn't let herself watch Gianna leave, even if it was to see her ass jiggle as she moved.

CHAPTER 10

Megan screamed, pumping her right arm in the air. "Get her! Faster! Faster!"

But Helen didn't seem to hear her. Or more likely, Helen could hear her, but that didn't actually make her legs move any faster or any more likely to knock down the other team's blocker. Helen was stopped again and again, and the other team's jammer was speeding past her, Gayle, and the rest of the team on the track.

Megan groaned and sat back in frustration even as the rest of the audience erupted in cheers. The other team's jammer had made it through, the first lead jammer of the game, and Helen followed it up with a spectacular fall.

Thankfully, the fall just looked dramatic, and Helen got up quickly, grinning and waving at the crowd. She pushed past the pack and spun her wheels down the track, trying to overtake the other team's jammer, but she wasn't quite fast enough.

Megan itched to be back on the track. She'd gone almost a week without any skating. She'd seen the doctor the day before, and the doctor had said she could skate slowly, so—after making Megan swear up and down she was telling the truth about the doctor's orders—Shelly had let her take a couple of laps before tonight's game. But now that the game had started, she was benched, and all she could do was watch her team play and feel incredibly frustrated that she wasn't joining them.

She'd come to the practices (partly to support her team, partly to at least see what they were doing, and partly because she had nothing else to do with her evenings), but those hadn't been nearly as frustrating. She loved skating, but what she really loved about roller derby was the adrenaline—the fight. That was what she was missing tonight.

She didn't *have* to be missing it, of course.

Gianna was in the audience, too; Megan had seen her when the team had skated out, before she sat down. She wondered whether Rolling in the Streets didn't have a game tonight, but of course, most teams didn't have a match every *single* Saturday night.

She hated the idea of Gianna missing a derby match to come see her. The idea was ridiculous—Gianna knew where she lived and where she worked; she could have come to visit any time during the week—but it stuck with her nonetheless.

Helen was passing the other team's jammer now, having passed half the pack. Megan yelled and screamed, but her heart wasn't in it as much.

Seconds later, the jam ended with the teams tied, 5-5. It was a promising start. Megan knew her team could win without her; it meant a little more work for the other jammers, but with her out, there were still thirteen people to take their turns on the track. They were all good skaters, and they could do it without her.

She just wished they didn't have to.

She glanced over her shoulder at Gianna, who was cheering with the rest of the crowd as the teams took their places for the next jam, then turned back quickly so she wouldn't see her looking. Gianna obviously knew she was there, but hadn't tried to speak to her.

They hadn't seen each other since the hospital. They'd texted a little bit—Gianna had offered to come over and help Megan out, but she turned down the offer. Apparently Gianna hadn't been offended by that, because they'd been trading some light banter every day since.

Megan did have to wonder why Gianna wasn't more upset. Megan had practically accused her of being just like her abusive ex. But maybe Gianna was really angry, and that's why she hadn't come to see Megan. Until now.

Or maybe Gianna was just being polite and respecting Megan's wishes.

She wished she wouldn't.

Her stomach twisted with guilt as she tried to focus on the match. Or was that more anxiety about not being out there? She was rolling her feet back and forth in her skates, wishing she could push away from the bench and onto the track, but she knew that would only be trouble.

Kristine was playing jammer now and doing better than Helen had. Her short stature was an advantage Megan never had. That was something fun to watch.

Megan was able to lose herself in derby for the rest of the game—until halftime came, and with it the break. She slumped back in her seat as the crowd surged around her. Even if she felt like eating, there was no way she could push through the crowd to get some snacks with her injured arm.

A hand came down hard on her uninjured shoulder, making her jump. "What the hell are you doing on skates?"

Gianna. Megan turned around and gave her stare back for her heavy-browed stare. "I saw the doctor yesterday. She said skating slowly was okay. I'm healing well."

"And you've been listening to the doctor?"

"Yes. Shelly wouldn't let me on skates until today. And she would hardly believe me at first. I should've gotten a damn note."

She wanted to sound bitter, furious that Gianna's interference was keeping her off her skates and out of the match. But she just sounded petulant. Like a child. Gianna probably got that all the time. A kindergarten teacher would know just how to deal with it.

But Gianna just sat down behind Megan. "I'm glad you're healing. I hope it keeps it up. It's strange to see you benched at a match."

Megan looked away. "It's strange for me, too."

"Do you blame me?" In the crowd noise, Gianna's voice was quiet enough to almost be lost.

But Megan had heard it, and she didn't want to pretend otherwise. "No. I know you didn't mean it."

"Is that what your ex used to say after she hit you?"

Megan winced. "No. She—sometimes, she'd say I... Yes." She didn't want to get into it, especially not here, in the middle of the crowd. Her inability to get on the track and help win the game echoed the powerlessness she'd felt in her relationship with Cari.

But it was true. Sometimes, Cari had said that. Megan hadn't meant to echo her words.

"She was lying." Gianna's voice was so soft that it *would* have been lost in the crowd noise if she hadn't leaned forward to whisper in Megan's ear. "I'm telling you the truth. I mean everything I say, even if not everything I do on skates, babe."

"I know." Megan wasn't sure if Gianna had heard her. The crowd was settling down. The match was about to start again.

When she looked back again, just as the whistle blew, Gianna was no longer behind her.

CHAPTER 11

At least Megan's Sunday routine didn't have to change due to injury. Like always, she was in pajamas (a loose T-shirt and shorts), eating takeout because she couldn't do much cooking, and watching Netflix. And drinking beer. Tara had brought her a consolatory six-pack, and she hadn't felt like touching any of it until today.

She'd gone to the afterparty the night before, but hadn't enjoyed herself. Gianna hadn't come; of course, since her team wasn't playing that night, she probably hadn't been invited.

Megan wasn't sure whether talking some more would have helped or not. What she really wanted was for Gianna to apologize for taking over, and she hadn't yet.

Gianna was probably waiting for Megan to apologize

for having Shelly drive her home. But that wasn't going to happen.

She was almost done with her fourth beer and her third season of Orphan Black when her phone chimed at her. She picked it up to see a new text notification from a number that wasn't in her contacts. She was just tipsy enough to swipe it open to see the full text.

Hi. I know it's been a while. I've been having a hard time.

Megan paused her show and stared at the text. Was it Gianna? Not unless she had a new number. Who would be texting her so familiarly when she didn't know their number?

Her eyes flicked up to the number at the top of the screen. It looked familiar, but she never memorized people's numbers, just put them in her contacts. Who could it be?

Maybe it was a wrong number.

She kept staring at the phone until another text appeared. *But I'm ready to forgive you. I know you didn't mean it.*

Her heart stuttered.

Cari.

She'd deleted the number from her contacts the day after Cari left, realizing she wasn't coming back. Megan didn't want to leave herself the temptation of texting Cari and begging. Obviously, Cari hadn't done the same thing. So she'd *chosen* not to contact Megan.

Until today.

Megan put her phone down to try to allow herself to think, but she just stared at an old derby poster she had framed on her wall, not taking any of it in. What did Cari want? To forgive her, of course. But why now? And did she really want forgiveness?

She had no idea what to say. *Yes, actually I meant it*? *Thanks* followed by an emoji that would accurately encapsulate her feelings?

There was no emoji for that.

Once again, her phone chimed while she was trying (and failing) to think. She couldn't help looking at it again.

Meet up tonight? I'll come to Zonia Cantina around 6. We can talk.

Megan took a shaky breath. Now she had to respond. She could ignore it until later and pretend that she just hadn't been paying attention to her phone, but Cari knew her better than that—she always had her phone on her. Unless she was playing roller derby. She could give that as her excuse for taking a long time to respond.

She glanced at her shoulder. But Cari would see the sling and want to know what was going on, and then Megan would have to tell her that she hadn't really been at practice.

And Cari would use the injury as another excuse to try to get her to quit roller derby.

Megan flattened her lips, picked up her phone, and typed out a response. *No. It's over. I meant it when I hit you back.*

Then she deleted the whole thing without sending it and sat back on the couch, staring at the ceiling.

She hadn't actually meant it. She hadn't even known what she was doing. It was just that one night Cari was yelling at her for coming home late from derby practice. Megan had been pissed, because Cari's anger was unreasonable. Derby sometimes ran late. There was nothing she could do about it. And it was too important for her to leave early.

"More important than me?" Cari had screamed.

"Yes," Megan had said, not thinking, just reacting.

Cari had slapped her in the face. It wasn't the first time, and it wasn't the worst she'd done. But this time Megan had reacted, too tired to think, still revved up from practice.

She'd swung out with her elbow, her pointy, bony elbow, which she couldn't use in roller derby—and slammed Cari in the stomach with it.

Cari had staggered back several steps, bumping into the refrigerator, where she'd claimed Megan's dinner was waiting. Megan just stood there for a moment, stunned and horrified at what she'd done.

But when she tried to run forward, to apologize and see whether there would be a bruise, Cari had shoved her away. She'd grabbed her jacket and her purse, leaving behind the cake she'd brought to share with Megan, and walked out.

It was their two-year anniversary.

Megan had run after her, but she hadn't looked back. She'd gotten in her car and driven away. Megan had texted her, then called her dozens of times that night, but she'd gotten no response.

The next night had been a Friday. She'd passed a miserable day at work, then gone back to trying to contact Cari. By the end of the night, though, she realized that Cari was not going to respond to her; she had left for good. She'd deleted Cari's number.

She'd been even more intense than usual the next day at practice, and they'd won that night's game by a significant margin. Shelly had pulled her aside to congratulate her, but warn her that if she continued playing with such intensity, she was going to hurt herself. That was when Megan had broken down and told her that she'd split up with her girlfriend.

She didn't tell anyone about the hitting. That was too much. She wasn't ready to have her friends look at her differently.

She knew she shouldn't have done it. She could have really hurt Cari that way. It was a total overreaction, and she'd been sick about it for weeks.

Megan realized that she was crying, even just remembering that time. She had to talk to Cari. If only to just get some closure, to make sure Cari really meant it. That would be enough.

She picked up her phone. *OK,* she texted. *I'll see you then.*

Megan tried to be late, to pretend that she didn't have a care in the world and that Cari was far down her priorities list, but when she arrived at Zonia Cantina—dressed in one of Cari's favorite dresses, despite the fiddly zipper, and with no makeup on—she glanced at the clock and saw that she was ten minutes early.

The bar was four blocks from Megan's apartment, not the nearest bar, but the best one within a mile's walk. She and Cari had been here a lot when they were together. It was a good place to meet and talk, with good drinks.

Right now she wondered if it was too close, or maybe too far away.

Cari wasn't there yet. Megan smoothed her dress nervously and sat at one of the tiny tables. A server Megan recognized came to take her order; she nearly ordered a beer, then realized she should have the greatest possible number of wits about her when talking to Cari, and ordered ginger ale instead.

As soon as the waitress left she wondered if she should have ordered food. It was dinnertime—had Cari been planning to eat here, or was it just drinks? When they'd been together, they'd usually come here after dinner. Megan wasn't hungry, since she'd been eating takeout all day, but maybe...

No. She was overthinking this. Even if she and Cari did end up ordering food, the polite thing to do would be to wait for Cari anyway.

She took a deep breath, wiped her sweaty palms on her

dress, and kept an eye on the door, trying to act calm for when Cari arrived.

A woman at the bar got up and walked past her, smiling and putting a swish in her step as she approached. Megan just stared blankly at her. The woman's smile faded, and she passed without comment.

Of course, the woman had been trying to flirt. Megan felt like smacking herself in the head. With Cari on the mind, she hadn't even thought about other girls.

But it was for the best that she not flirt back. Right now she couldn't handle any kind of encounter with another woman.

Her ginger ale arrived. She didn't drink any of it. What would Cari think when she saw Megan with something nonalcoholic? Would she see Megan as weak, unable to handle talking to her?

Maybe she should order a drink. She tried to remember what the wine that Gianna had ordered for them had been. But they probably wouldn't have that here.

Before she could think herself into oblivion on that question, the door swung open and Cari walked inside. She spotted Megan immediately, smiling and walking toward her. Megan felt her heart flutter as she stood automatically.

Cari reached out, and Megan took her hand. Cari squeezed it. "I'm happy to see you again, Meggie." The same pet name she'd always used. It felt like she was squeezing

Megan's heart as well as her hand when she said it. Megan could only swallow and nod.

They sat down, and Cari glanced around, then turned back to Megan. "I'm sorry I was out of touch for so long, but... well, you can understand my reaction, I hope."

Megan nodded again. "Of course." Her voice sounded hoarse.

A million other responses were going through her head. *Obviously, I can't understand it, because I didn't leave any of the times you hit me. No, I can't understand, because I only gave you what I was getting. Golden rule, right? Yes, absolutely, I understand leaving me without a word. I just love it when girls do that to me.*

But she didn't say any of them.

"It's been really difficult," Cari continued. "I didn't know if I could ever get past what you did to me. Time has helped, though."

"Time apart." Megan was starting to feel sick. Had Cari not even meant to dump her, just take a break? Would that make what she'd done with Gianna cheating?

"Yes." The waitress returned, and Cari ordered a cocktail. So she hadn't come for dinner. Good. But she was perfectly willing to drink hard liquor. She wasn't planning to leave anytime soon.

Maybe she wasn't planning to drive at all the rest of the evening.

"I know it's been hard for you, too," Cari said. "But all is forgiven now, all right?" She smiled and held her hand out across the table.

Megan reached out and took her hand, but she didn't say anything. She didn't know if she could.

Agreeing that all was forgiven would mean that she was forgiving Cari, too. She wasn't ready to do that. She didn't know if she ever would be. Could you forgive someone for something they weren't sorry for?

Megan had apologized over and over again, but that was months ago now. She wasn't sorry anymore. Or was she?

In her pocket, her phone buzzed. She glanced at it, but didn't take it out. She hoped it wasn't Bonnie again. That was the last person she could deal with right now.

Cari was still smiling at her, but the smile had begun to look a bit fixed. She was waiting for Megan's response.

"I'll forgive you if you can genuinely apologize," Megan said.

The smile slipped a bit. Cari's eyes narrowed. "Didn't I already?"

"You apologized for being out of touch." And Megan didn't even know if she'd meant it. Was it a real apology when you followed it right up with an excuse and complaints about how difficult it had been for you?

"I'm sorry I left without a word. I'm sorry I got so angry. I know I was overreacting." Cari squeezed her hand. "We have to talk about that roller derby stuff, though. Is that what happened to your arm?"

"Yes. It's not as bad as it looks." Megan had almost forgotten about her injury.

The waitress came with Cari's drink, and she let go of Megan's hand to sip it. Megan took the opportunity to quickly slip her phone out of her pocket. Two texts from Gianna appeared on her screen.

Are you doing OK?

I'm not giving you up this easily. Please talk to me.

"Meggie, I'm trying to talk to you. Save the phone for later."

Megan hastily shoved her phone back into her pocket, her heart beating hard. Cari had put down her drink and her eyes were flashing. "Sorry."

"Who was it?"

"Someone from roller derby." It wasn't entirely true, but it wasn't entirely a lie, either. And none of her possible answers would mollify Cari.

If she'd said it was Bonnie or one of her parents, that would have been all right (though Cari and Bonnie had always hated each other). But it would also have been a complete lie, and she didn't know if that was worth it. Cari would find out eventually that she was lying, and then there would be...

Would there be? Maybe it would be different now. Maybe Cari really meant that she was sorry and that she would come back.

Cari smiled and shook her head. "It's my own fault for

being away for so long. You've had to find other people to talk to. But I'm back now."

"You're back," Megan said slowly. "But are you back the same as you were before? Is anything going to change?"

Cari's smile broadened and she reached toward Megan again. "No, Meggie, sweetheart. Everything can be just the same as it was. But I hope you're taking a break from roller derby with that injury."

Megan didn't take her hand. There was another lump in her throat. Cari had seen the injury, but hadn't said anything until she found an excuse to blame it on roller derby. It could have been from anything—Megan could have been in a car accident or fallen off a trampoline.

Gianna had texted to see if she was all right even though she'd just seen her yesterday, even though Megan had pushed her away, even though she'd refused to have anything official between them.

And Cari had obviously, completely, misunderstood Megan's question. Or at least she'd misunderstood the intent. Megan couldn't let everything be the same as it had been. She couldn't live that way. She wouldn't let herself.

Besides, roller derby had made her stronger. Not just physically, but also emotionally, surer in her own skin. The next time someone hit her would be just like the last time: she would hit back.

Megan looked straight at Cari, lifting her shoulders into a defensive, powerful stance that she'd learned at roller derby. It hurt, and she shouldn't have done it, but it made her feel stronger.

"You might not have noticed," she said, "but I'm not apologizing."

Cari blinked, but her smile didn't fade. "You don't have to apologize, Meggie. Everything's going to be all right."

Megan shook her head. "I didn't apologize because I'm not sorry. You do that again—you lay another fucking finger on me—and I'll hit you back even harder."

For a moment Cari's smile was frozen on her face. Then it transformed into a snarl of pure rage. "You bitch! You just invited me here to lead me on, didn't you?"

"No. You aren't even worth that." Megan made sure to enunciate every word as she stood up. "I came here because you wanted to apologize, and I was so damn depressed from my shoulder injury that I thought it would be good to see you. But it wasn't. It was the same as it always was."

Cari shot to her feet, hands white-knuckled on the table. "I love you and you know you love me. We can't be apart any longer. You need me!"

Megan remembered Cari as exuding strength and power, even though she was, like Gianna, several inches shorter than Megan. But she didn't feel that power anymore. Cari was angry, but her anger was petty.

She reached into her purse for cash and tossed a five on the table, to pay for her untouched ginger ale and hopefully make up for the scene they were causing. "You're the last thing I need, Cari. Goodbye. I mean it. Don't you touch me again."

She left the bar.

Her hand was shaking as she reached into her purse again. It took her three tries to unlock her phone. But she did it and, with adrenaline still pumping through her body, her ears roaring with the anger and daring of what she'd just done, she blocked Cari's number and deleted all of her texts.

Then, as she walked the blocks home, she texted Gianna.

I'm OK. Thanks for texting. It actually was just what I needed.

The reply was swift. *Good. Can I come over? I'll bring food.*

Megan took a deep breath and leaned on the door to her building while she considered. She wanted Gianna right now; the fight with Cari didn't feel over, and it never would, now that she didn't even know if Cari was going to try to contact her. She couldn't afford to try to get closure with Cari, so she wanted the next best thing.

But at the same time, she wanted to be alone. She wanted to mentally explore being alone, and single, and not looking. And she was drained from the fight; she needed to relax.

Reluctantly, she began to climb the stairs, and texted back. *Not tonight. Sorry. I need some time alone.*

That sounded like she was rejecting Gianna. Quickly, she typed a follow-up text. *We'll talk soon, k?*

The pause was longer this time, long enough for her to put away her phone, unlock her door, and put her things down. Then the phone buzzed again.

Sure you're OK?

Yes, I'm sure, Megan texted back. *Doing a lot better. Thank you. I mean it.*

Let me know if you need anything.

Megan smiled. *I will.*

Then she wriggled uncomfortably out of the dress while trying to keep her shoulder immobilized and tossed it in a wrinkled heap on the floor of her closet. Who needed dresses when there was derby?

CHAPTER 12

On Monday, during her lunch break, Megan texted Gianna the whole story of her encounter with Cari the night before. Looking back on it, she found it kind of funny, especially her dramatic exit.

But she was proud of herself. She'd made a choice this time—the right choice. When she'd hit Cari back, that hadn't been making a conscious choice. It was just that her girlfriend instinct—her submission instinct—had finally lost out to the new roller-derby instinct. Cari had been the one to do the leaving.

This time she'd done the leaving, and it felt good.

It was nice to hear that Gianna was proud of her, too.

Megan wanted to tell everyone at roller derby the next night, especially Shelly, but stopped before she could say anything. She'd forgotten that Gianna was the only one she'd told the truth about Cari to. If she was going to explain how she'd stood up for herself to anyone else, she would have to give the backstory first.

Being unable to play derby was bad enough. She'd face up to telling that story another time, when she was stronger.

She kept up the texting with Gianna over the next two days, just light banter for the most part, nothing else serious. Gianna hinted that she wanted an apology, but Megan wouldn't let herself think about it. She wasn't going to apologize for things that weren't her fault. She wouldn't ask for forgiveness.

And then, on Thursday morning, she got in to work to find a flood.

Something had broken in the lobby bathrooms. Karen and Joe were standing over the puddles, screaming about whose fault it was. Megan found the mop, cleaned up the spill, and turned off the water under each of the sinks and toilets, all of which seemed to be overflowing—clean water, thank all the gods.

"Call a fucking plumber!" Karen was screaming at Joe, her face red.

"I'll call the plumber," Megan said. "Do we have a plumber?"

"Do I look like I know any plumbers?" Joe shouted toward Karen, but he might as well have been talking to Megan.

"Google it is, then," Megan said, and sat down behind her desk.

The first two plumbers she called couldn't get anyone out that day (but at least Joe and Karen moved to their office and lowered the volume of their argument). The third could, but not until evening, and it would cost double. While Megan argued with the plumber, holding the phone uncomfortably to her face with her right shoulder, she frantically tried to look through the books to see whether they had the extra money to cover it. She did not see a budget item for repairs—but she didn't keep the books, so she could be missing anything.

She was still on the phone when the front door opened and she looked up automatically.

Black hair. Curves. A red, red smile. Gianna was there.

Megan stared, her heart suddenly beating double-time and her face draining of all its blood. What was Gianna doing here? She couldn't deal with her. Not this, not on top of everything else.

Then two little boys walked in holding hands, and Megan bit back a curse. How could she have forgotten? This was the day of Gianna's class field trip.

"I'll call you back," she told the plumber, and flung the phone back onto its cradle. More little kids in pairs, and several adults, were following Gianna in. Joe and Karen had stopped shouting, but the door to their office was still open.

She had to act normal. She had to pretend Gianna was just another customer. She had to make sure they didn't all demand their money back for showing up on this perfectly shitty day.

"Hi," Gianna said, smiling at her—not one of her saucy or belligerent smiles, but a perky one with an edge of sweetness. "I made a reservation a while back. It should be under Gianna Esposito."

She was being normal, too. That made it easier for Megan to be normal right back.

"I remember you, of course," she said. "No need to look it up. First of all, I'm sorry to have to tell you that our lobby restrooms are out of order." She raised her voice to make sure all the chaperones, who were trying to get the kids to quiet down, could hear her. "There's another—just a moment."

She took a deep breath, composed herself, and then dashed into the office, closing the door behind her. Joe was sitting behind his desk; Karen was standing over it, hands on her hips. She turned her face, still red, to Megan. "Get back out there," she snapped.

"Did anyone check the bathrooms in the back?" she asked desperately. "We have a class full of kindergarteners here and if none of the restrooms are working, they might have to leave."

"I went this morning," Joe said. "They're working fine. No flooding."

"Great," Megan said, giving him a relieved smile. At least one of them thought of these things.

The smile he gave her back made her skin crawl. As she turned away, Karen was already hissing angrily at him. This time Megan shut the office door behind her.

"I was just checking on things," she said. "There's another set of restrooms in the back of the trampoline park—you'll see the signs when you get inside."

"Can I take Parker and Shelby there right now?" asked a black man who looked young except for the gray in his temples, pointing to two little girls, holding hands and poking at each other. "I think they need it quickly."

"Yes, of course." Megan hurried out from behind the desk and opened a drawer on the side of the room. Pulling out the socks was awkward with one arm, but she'd learned to do it. "We just ask that you wear our trampoline socks before entering the room. Here are two in kids' sizes, and one for adults." She handed them over, avoiding Gianna's eyes. "You can put them on over regular socks if you want, or take your socks off first—we do wash these. Make sure you take your shoes off, though."

The man squatted down with the little girls and then began helping them with their shoes and socks. Megan straightened her back and took a deep breath. Her spiel was all out of whack, but that wasn't Gianna's fault—or even the fault of the plumbing. She should have expected it from the moment she booked a party of kindergarteners.

She tried to count, but the little kids kept moving around, and then Parker and Shelby disappeared with their chaperone, and she lost track. "Forty-one including the kids, right?" she muttered to Gianna. It was a relief to be able to look at her, to put on her customer-service smile and keep everything normal.

"Forty-two of us today, actually," Gianna said with a grimace. "Thirty kids, eleven parents, and me. You can just charge the same card I gave you, right?"

"Absolutely. Help me hand out the socks?"

Between the two of them, they got enough pairs of socks handed out for each parent and each kid. One of the kids threw the socks on the floor and started screaming that he didn't want to wear them. Gianna immediately squatted down in front of him and started making soothing noises. Megan stared in mild astonishment. Gianna really looked and sounded like a kindergarten teacher—clearly still the same person as on the roller-derby track, but with a whole new attitude.

This must be how Gianna had felt seeing Megan here the first time.

A little girl walked up to Megan, holding her trampoline socks. She still had little purple anklets on, but no shoes. "Miss, will you help me?"

Megan stared at her, totally at a loss. She did not deal with kids—their parents did that when they came to the trampoline park. But this girl was so cute, with her pigtails and her lisping politeness.

"Okay." Megan took the socks and squatted down. The little girl promptly sat on the floor, her feet straight out in front of her.

"Did you want to leave your regular socks on?" Megan asked. The little girl just stared at her silently. Megan didn't want to pull her socks off without permission, so she lifted the girl's foot and started to tug the trampoline sock on over it. It was slow going with just one hand, and the child wasn't helping.

"Bella! You didn't need to ask the nice lady for help. I'll do that." Gianna came striding over, squatted down, and pulled the trampoline sock out of Megan's unresisting hand. "Sorry about that," she said over her shoulder, obviously to Megan but without using her name. "Don't you have things you should be doing? Come on, sweetie, it'll be easier with your socks off." The last was to the kid. It was amazing how seamlessly she switched.

Megan heard a click behind her as she stood up, and she turned, but nothing had changed. Joe or Karen must have opened the door and decided not to face the chaos of thirty kindergarteners.

She stood still, disoriented for a moment, then remembered what Gianna had said. Things she should be doing, right.

"Anyone who's got their trampoline socks on?" she called over the general noise. Several heads popped up and a few kids' hands raised. "Okay. Get your shoes and socks and put them on the shelves." She pointed to rows of wooden shelves under the drawer. "Make sure you keep your stuff together and keep track of where you left them so it's easy to find them again."

The room devolved back into chaos, but the chaperones seemed to be doing okay showing the kids what to do. Megan retreated back behind the desk to catch her breath.

She was supposed to be doing some salesy talk now too, but screw it. The kids didn't care and the parents couldn't listen.

When she saw the two little girls return from the bathroom with their chaperone, she made sure they knew what to do with their shoes. Then Gianna popped up again in front of her desk.

"They're almost done. I assume you have some kind of safety lecture."

Megan nodded, looking at all the kids with some dismay. "Are they going to listen?"

Gianna smiled again. "They will. I'll calm them down."

She really loved the kids, Megan realized. She had to, to organize a trip like this for them. It was strange to see, and sweet.

A few moments later, Gianna clapped her hands twice, and the room got significantly quieter, with most of the kids turning toward her. "Everybody find your buddies and line up," she called. "Miss Megan is going to tell you all how to stay safe and not hurt yourselves inside."

Miss Megan? It sounded so gentle and respectful. Megan liked it.

She was astonished at how quickly the kids lined themselves up, holding hands with their partners. The parents spaced themselves out at intervals behind the line.

Megan cleared her throat and went through her safety list, telling them to keep their socks on, to avoid the edges of the trampolines when jumping, and to be careful of everyone else. She told the parents where the weight limits on the smaller trampolines were listed and how to find the black-light room. She figured the kids could find out about the other themed rooms themselves—it might be more fun as a surprise.

"Miss Megan," one of the little boys shouted.

She almost blushed hearing the name coming out of the kids. It was so cute, but so strange. "Yes, did you have a question?"

"Did you break your arm falling off of a tram-poh-line?"

Gianna, at the back of the line, covered her face with her hand; Megan could tell she was trying not to laugh. Megan was having a hard time keeping a straight face herself. She couldn't explain to these kids about roller derby, but she didn't want to lie and tell them she'd fallen off a trampoline, either. And explaining that her arm wasn't broken was just too complicated.

"No, I didn't. I fell down when I was roller skating. But that just shows that you should be careful, okay? You can hurt yourself even when it seems safe."

The little boy nodded, his eyes wide. His buddy shook their joined hands, and he finally said, "Okay."

"Any other questions?" She didn't give them time to think. "Okay, that's everything, so have fun!" She opened the door. They ran inside, screams giving voice to their joy. Even the parents looked excited as they followed the kids in.

Only Gianna lingered.

"Go on, have fun in there with them," Megan said, sitting down at her desk with a thump. She smiled weakly, knowing she was going to have to get back on the phone with the plumbers. "You have to chaperone your group, and I have to find someone to come fix the bathrooms."

"Do you have to do everything around here?"

Megan shrugged—one shoulder. She'd mostly gotten used to keeping the left one still.

"What about those people?" Gianna asked, lifting her arm to gesture at Joe and Karen's closed door. "What do they do?"

"They're the owners. You really do have to go chaperone your group. It's a rule."

Gianna frowned at her. "Are you really okay?"

"I am, I promise. But thanks for asking."

"Okay." Gianna nodded. "I have a match Saturday night, but I'll come to the Monstrous match if mine ends early enough, all right? I know you're going to be miserable sitting there watching again."

"You don't have to do that." Megan smiled again, this time with more strength behind it. She wanted Gianna to come, even if everyone else would think it was strange that another player had shown up. She could live with that. She could live with a lot, if it meant Gianna was with her.

Gianna grabbed Megan's hand where it lay on the desk by her computer mouse. "I want to. I'll see you then."

Megan squeezed Gianna's hand back, then watched her head into the trampoline park. It felt like they'd just made up, even though neither of them had apologized or offered forgiveness.

They would probably have to do a lot more talking. But right now, they were just fine.

CHAPTER 13

It was the worst roller derby match Megan had ever watched—because she was forced to watch it, while being sure that if she were playing, they would be winning, not losing.

She had to admire Manson Girl, a jammer on the opposing team; she was little and quick, with a lot of flexibility that let her get around blocks that would have hit a slower player. The other players on the other team were all good, but that one was the best.

The fact that they were playing against an amazing jammer didn't lessen the pain when she kept bringing the other team ahead in points—especially when Megan tried to use both hands to cheer and was reminded by the twinge in her shoulder that she really shouldn't be doing that.

At work and at home she'd gotten good at keeping her shoulder immobile, but here at the derby track she seemed to have a hard time remembering her injury. At least she was off the painkillers now, and she would see the doctor next week, when she would hopefully be fully healed and ready to play again.

And Gianna had just sat down behind her, two jams from the end of the game. Megan hadn't turned around to see her, but she knew the sudden warmth at her back could only come from one person.

The next jam went well; Helen was nearly as quick as the other team's jammer, and the Monstrous Regiment blockers acquitted themselves nearly as well, keeping the other jammer (not Manson Girl) at bay. Megan cheered when the jam ended with Monstrous Regiment nearly caught up to the other team. Behind her, she could hear Gianna cheering as well.

For the last jam, though, the other team fielded Manson Girl again, and while Shelly put Tara on the track, she had to keep Gayle, their best blocker, back—she'd played in more than half the jams and was exhausted. The match ended with Monstrous Regiment losing by five points.

Megan groaned and sat back in her seat, covering her face with her right hand. They'd been so close. The rest of the crowd was screaming, but she just couldn't join in.

She felt hot breath on her ear a moment before hearing a shout into it. "You guys would have won if you'd been on the track."

"I know," Megan said, then turned to grin at Gianna. "But thanks for saying so."

The other girls were skating back to the locker rooms as the crowd noise quieted. Megan stood up to join them, and Gianna caught her arm. "Hey, babe, want to go out for ice cream? You probably shouldn't be drinking, with your arm, but you need something."

Megan barely considered for a second. "Ice cream sounds perfect. I'll meet you out back?"

Gianna nodded and let go of her arm. Megan skated slowly to the locker room, already imagining Gianna with chocolate sauce dripping down her... well, that wasn't going to happen in the ice cream parlor.

The locker room was full of a low buzz about the game. They were already going over tactics, thinking of how they could do better next time. Megan joined in as she began the slow process of removing her skates one-handed.

"Let me help," Kristine said, squatting down in front of her. She loosened the laces quickly and efficiently.

"Thanks," Megan said with feeling. "I can't wait until I can do it properly myself." She pulled her feet out of the skates and stuck them into the slip-on shoes she'd been wearing every day.

"Are you coming to the afterparty?" Kristine asked as she stood up with Megan's skates, replacing them in her bag. "I know you missed it last week."

Megan shook her head. "I'm going out for ice cream." She stumbled over her words a little, not sure who to say she was going with—Mountain Bruise or Gianna—and ending up with nothing at all.

Kristine's eyes widened. "Ooh, that sounds like an even better idea. Can I come with?"

"Where are you going?" asked Mindy.

"Ice cream," Kristine said.

"Oh, I'll drive," said Helen, leaning toward them.

Megan sat tongue-tied as they agreed among themselves to come with her for ice cream. They probably half felt they were doing her a favor and half actually wanted ice cream. She had no idea how to tell them that it was actually, sort of, a date—with someone from the other team she'd been seeing in secret.

Screw secrets. She stood up, grabbing her bag. "I'm actually going with Gianna. From Rolling in the Streets."

They all stared at her. "The one who skated into your shoulder?" Helen asked.

Megan swallowed, hiding her wince. Of course they would think of that first. "Uh, yeah. We've been sort of seeing each other."

That was a terrible description, but she didn't need to go into detail.

Or maybe she did. They were still staring at her as though unable to believe that she could possibly want to date Gianna. But it didn't matter. She was doing what she wanted to do, and it didn't matter what anyone else thought. She turned and headed for the door.

"Hey." Shelly had been talking to Gayle, touched her elbow as she walked past. "Are you pissed?"

"No." Megan forced a smile, aware that being unable to

smile naturally wasn't helping her case. "We lost, but that wasn't the fault of anybody on this team. Well, maybe you for keeping Gayle off the track during the last jam."

Gayle rolled her eyes, placing her hands on her hips. "That's what I was saying."

"It's not worth winning if another one of our best players gets injured," Shelly said with exasperation. It sounded like they'd been having this argument for a while.

"I'll be healed up soon," Megan promised. "And the season's almost over. But anyway, I'm heading out."

"Skipping the afterparty again?" Shelly raised her eyebrows.

Megan took a deep breath. "I'm actually going for ice cream with Gianna."

"Oh!" Shelly grinned. So did Gayle.

"Have a great time," Gayle said with a wink.

"Yeah. See you guys on Tuesday." Megan walked out before they could make any more comments, feeling a little depressed again. She would love to have sex with Gianna, but didn't even know if that would be possible, with her arm.

Gianna was leaning against her car door with her keys in her hand when Megan finally made it out of the building. "There you are, babe."

"I wasn't trying to ditch you," Megan said, answering what she was sure was an unspoken question. She liked being with Gianna too much to let Gianna doubt that. "I sort of got ambushed by my team. Some of them tried to invite themselves along, but I told them... well, I told people we'd been seeing each other."

Gianna's eyes lit up and she quickly turned away, unlocking her door and getting inside, then leaning across the seat to open Megan's door as well. When Megan got in the car, her face was calm again. "I guess that's progress," she said.

"Sure." Megan closed her door and buckled herself in, feeling uncertain again. Gianna wanted her to say they were together—that much was obvious. But what if Megan could never get to that point? Was she just going to wait around forever?

Gianna hit the accelerator, and Megan winced as she was tossed backward in the seat. Normally she didn't mind the way Gianna drove, but... "Can you drive a little more gently today? Just while my shoulder is healing?"

"Oh. Yeah, of course." Gianna glanced sideways at Megan, biting her lower lip, and slowed down a bit.

Megan felt bad—she was sure they were thinking of the same thing, the way Megan had mocked Gianna's driving that night at the hospital. She'd meant it to be teasing and lighthearted, as usual, but it hadn't come out right.

Thankfully, as they made to pull out onto the road, a car came flying past, wailing its horn at them. Gianna shouted curses after it and flipped it the bird, an obscene gesture that she somehow seemed to make with her whole body. Megan started laughing, and that defused the tension.

It was a short ride to the ice cream place, but a long line—the day had been nice and warm, but the leaves were turning, and soon the shop would be closed for the winter. Megan saw two little kids pulling on their parent's hands and was reminded of two days before.

"So the kids liked the trampoline park?" she asked, as much for the sake of having something to talk about as anything else.

Gianna grinned immediately, her whole face turning sunny. Megan loved that grin—just as bright and wide as any she showed at roller derby, but without the triumph or competitiveness. It was just pure joy.

"They loved it," she said. "Are you kidding? They couldn't stop talking about it all day Friday. They've already asked me twice if they can do another field trip there."

Megan laughed with delight. She'd figured the kids would love it, but when they left they'd been whining and dragging their feet, some even crying. They had probably just been tired—and maybe mad that they had to leave the trampoline park. "Well, anytime you want to set up another party, just let me know. Weekdays during the school year are always slow."

Gianna shook her head as they inched forward in line. "I don't know if the parents will go for another one. It's a lot more expensive than our usual field trips."

"The parents who came seemed to like the idea. A lot of them took brochures or flyers." Megan thought back to Thursday afternoon, picturing the parents who'd taken flyers. "Actually, I think all of them did. And three of them thanked me specifically. That's really the best kind of day, when the customers are so happy."

"That reminds me, did you get the bathrooms fixed?"

"Yeah, I had to come in an hour early yesterday to meet the plumber, but it was fine. I got paid overtime and the bathroom got fixed. I haven't been sleeping well without the exercise from derby anyway." With a grimace, she gestured at her shoulder.

The bell on the front door rang softly, and she glanced back. *Oh, no.* It seemed that Kristine, Mindy, and Helen had decided to come for ice cream after all, and they'd already spotted Megan. Thankfully, a few other people were between them in line, but it was going to be hard to avoid them.

Gianna was talking again, and Megan quickly turned back to pay attention to her. "You never did answer me about what Joe and Karen do, babe."

Megan sighed. "They're the owners. They run the place."

Gianna shook her head. "You run the place." She jabbed her fingers toward Megan. "You talk to the customers, you run the payments, you call the plumber. What the hell do they do?"

"They do everything I do after regular business hours. Most people want to come to the trampoline park after work or on weekends."

"All right, so you don't have to do everything, but still, shouldn't the owners be the ones calling a plumber?"

"They don't know how much we can afford to pay a plumber."

"You keep the books, too?"

"Well, I—" Megan grimaced, closing her eyes for a moment. "Can we not talk about work anymore? It's stressing me out, and I thought we came here to enjoy ourselves."

"You didn't mind talking about work two minutes ago, when we were talking about the kids."

"Next!" shouted the bored-looking young woman behind the ice cream counter. Megan hurried forward so she didn't have to answer Gianna. Unfortunately, they'd been talking so much that she'd forgotten to think about her ice cream order, so she just hastily ordered a chocolate cone with sprinkles.

Gianna ordered a sundae and told the girl they were together, paying before Megan could say anything. Megan made a mental note to try to arrange payment ahead on their next date—Gianna was so much more forceful than her, and she seemed to care a lot about paying for Megan, but Megan didn't want to feel like she was always being treated.

Next date. Was she really thinking about that? Did this really count as a date?

They collected their ice cream when it was ready. Gianna silently pointed out an open table for two, and they pushed their way through the crowd toward it. "Roller derby comes in handy here," Gianna said over her shoulder, making Megan laugh.

But she also glanced back, looking for her friends. They had just reached the counter and were ordering. None of them was looking toward her; maybe they would sit in different parts of the shop. Megan wouldn't have to worry about them.

The chairs were spindly and narrow. Megan wasn't sure they could hold her narrow bulk, let alone Gianna's. But the curvy blocker sat with ease, even though her ass was spilling over the sides. She grinned wickedly at Megan. "Like what you see?"

"You know I do," Megan said, though she hastily sat down and stopped staring at Gianna's ass. Instead, she turned her attention to their ice cream. Gianna had scooped a large spoonful of vanilla ice cream and hot fudge sauce into her mouth already.

A little bit of chocolate was sliding down her lower lip. Megan stared again, transfixed. It was almost like her daydream.

"Now what are you looking at?" Gianna asked.

"There's some chocolate sauce on your lip," Megan said, gesturing toward the spot on her own face.

But instead of licking it off, Gianna leaned forward over her sundae. "Why don't you clean it off for me?" she purred.

Megan glanced nervously over at the counter, where the other derby girls were still waiting for their ice cream. But she'd already told them she was going to be here with Gianna. What was she so nervous about?

"Hey, babe," Gianna said. "You want this or not?"

"Yeah, this is stupid," Megan said. She bent forward and met Gianna's lips with hers, sucking off the chocolate sauce and experiencing a scorching kiss that made her tingle all over.

"What's so stupid?" Gianna asked, sitting back as though nothing of interest had happened. "You spilled some of your ice cream, by the way."

Megan looked at the table, where Gianna was gesturing, and wrinkled her nose. She hadn't held her cone properly, and some ice cream had dripped on the table. "What, you're not going to lick that up?"

Gianna laughed and tossed a napkin at Megan. She wiped it up and slurped at her cone, making sure none of the rest of it was going to spill.

"And don't let that distract you from answering," Gianna said, raising her eyebrows. "You've never been shy about kissing in public before."

"It's not that," Megan said, looking over her shoulder again. She could just see Kristine, Mindy, and Helen, crowded around another little table halfway across the room. "It's my friends. I guess I didn't want them to see us together. Like I said, it's stupid. I don't know why it took me so long to tell them I was dating you, either. No one cares if I'm fraternizing with the enemy."

Gianna snorted. "Took you long enough to figure that out."

"If I'm so stupid, why do you hang out with me?"

Gianna gave her spoon a long, exaggerated lick. "You have your charms."

"Like how I argue with you all the time."

Gianna grinned. "That's one of them."

Megan grinned back at her. "All right, tell me how stupid I am for caring what my friends think of my dating life."

Gianna waggled the spoon at her, then dove down into her sundae again. "You already figured that one out. I'm going to tell you how stupid you are for doing all the work at your job, instead."

"I already told you, I don't do everything. And I love my job."

Gianna shook her head and swallowed. "You just told me ten minutes ago that talking about work stressed you out."

Megan shrugged and bit the edge of her ice cream cone, crunching it between her teeth. She was annoyed, but she didn't want to stop arguing with Gianna. Like usual. "Everyone gets stressed out by work. You can't tell me you don't. My job is great, but it's still not roller derby."

"Even roller derby can be stressful."

"Exactly! Even if somehow roller derby was my job, it wouldn't be perfect."

"Yeah, but your job is a lot worse than not perfect, isn't it?" Gianna frowned, nibbling on the ice cream on her spoon.

"It's not that bad. Come on, I work in a trampoline park. I get to see happy people every day."

"And that's your favorite part of the job, right?"

"Of course. Who wouldn't like that best?"

"People who don't like having to deal with customers."

"They wouldn't want to work the front desk at a trampoline park." Megan pointed her half-eaten cone at Gianna, feeling like she'd scored a point.

"Yes, but maybe they would have to, and then they would look for another job that wasn't so dysfunctional."

"My job is perfectly functional."

"Yeah, because you do everything."

"You just agreed that I don't do everything!"

Gianna batted her eyelashes. "I thought you liked arguing with me."

"Yeah, but just contradicting me, or yourself, isn't arguing. I feel like I'm on Monty Python."

That made Gianna burst out laughing, and Megan couldn't help laughing, too, so that their argument devolved into giggles even as they finished their ice cream.

"All right, babe," Gianna said, leaning forward. Her hands were under the table, and she ran one of them up the inside of Megan's thigh, making her suck in her breath. "Let's go fraternize."

Megan glanced at her shoulder. "I'm not sure how much fraternizing I can do without moving my shoulder."

"I'm well aware of your limitations," Gianna said, her gaze running over Megan's shoulders and chest. She slid her hand back down Megan's thigh and away, then stood up. "Come on, I'm looking forward to the challenge."

Gianna took Megan back to her apartment and took off her clothes, one piece at a time, moving slowly and gently. Megan tried to give her advice and guidance, but every time she started to say something, Gianna would stop her with a kiss. Finally, she gave up. Gianna was doing a much better job not jostling her shoulder than she did herself, anyway.

The hard part was Megan herself—trying not to reach for Gianna with both arms. Gianna wasn't undressing herself, and Megan couldn't pull her clothes off with just one hand.

If she'd thought watching roller derby without playing because of her injury was frustrating, it was nothing to this.

"Gianna, come on," she whispered.

Gianna kissed her again, their mouths open and hot against each other, her hand sliding up underneath Megan's sling to caress her breasts. "Shh," she said into Megan's mouth. "This is all about you."

"But I don't want it to be," Megan said.

"Too bad, babe," Gianna said. "I'm in charge."

She put her hands on Megan's hips and started to turn her, but Megan stopped, bracing herself and putting her right arm out, pressing it against Gianna's breastbone. "No."

Gianna stopped, raising her eyebrows. "No?"

"You don't get to be in charge."

Gianna's mouth twitched into a slight smile. "It can't always be your turn."

Megan took a deep breath. "I have to have control, though. With Cari—my ex—I always let her take charge."

Gianna frowned. "How many times do I have to tell you I'm not her, and I'm not going to treat you like that, ever?"

"It's not about telling. Telling doesn't teach my subconscious anything." Megan shook her head, frustrated. She was totally killing the mood, but if Gianna kept pushing her around, the mood would have been killed anyway. "I have to know that I have the power. You have to show me."

Gianna put her hands on her hips, jutting her chin out so that her lower lip pouted. It was totally cute, but Megan wasn't about to tell her that. "Or maybe you have to learn that just because someone takes control during sex, or any other time, it doesn't mean they're trying to hurt you."

"You don't have to *try* to hurt me! Or what's this?" She pointed to her shoulder.

Gianna stepped back, her eyes wide. "I thought you didn't blame me for that!"

"I don't. It was an accident. I'm just saying, I have to be more careful now when I skate. Maybe you have to be more careful now when we have sex."

"What do you think I've been doing?" Gianna flung her arm toward the pile of clothes on the floor. "Maybe you just don't know how to be careful with yourself."

Megan looked at the clothes and grimaced, her anger fading as her shoulder gave a twinge to remind her that

Gianna had undressed her more successfully than she undressed herself. "Okay, you're right. Letting you take charge while you undressed me was easier."

"Easier isn't always better." Gianna stepped forward again, her curves lightly pressing against Megan's naked body. "I want to get this right, babe. I don't want to just say, okay, it's easier to do it this way, without fixing the underlying problem." She kissed her, her lips warm and soft.

Megan let herself enjoy the kiss for a moment, then broke away. "Why?"

"Why?" Gianna blinked at her, her lashes shadowing her eyes. "Why what?"

"Why do you want to get this right? Why not just go with what's easier in the moment?"

"Are you really asking that?"

"It's a genuine question."

"I want to be with you, Megan. I want this to last. I like being with you, and even if you're not ready to make a commitment, I'm willing to wait."

Megan sighed and rested her forehead against Gianna's. "I don't want to make you wait."

"Then make the commitment. Say you're mine." Gianna held very still.

"I don't want to lie to you, either."

"I was afraid you'd say that."

"So why do you still want me when I'm not willing to make a commitment to you?"

"You don't get it, do you?" Gianna stepped back and put

her hands—very lightly and gently—on Megan's shoulders. "It's not about the commitment. It's about you. If all we ever have is this, playing derby together and going on occasional dates and having awesome sex, then I'll accept that. And I want to make it last. I won't take shortcuts that might screw us, or you, up later."

"But why me?"

Gianna smiled and shook her head. "Because you're gorgeous and you're funny and we always have something to talk about. It also helps that you're an amazing roller-derby player."

Megan took a deep breath. She still didn't get why Gianna would want to date her over anyone else on their teams—Shelly or Tara or Britney Scares—but she could accept that. And she didn't think she'd have much success arguing with Gianna about her virtues.

But she didn't want to make Gianna wait around for something that might never happen, either.

"I have to be honest with you. I really like being with you, and everything about you, but I'm not in this for the same thing you are. I'm trying to be very true to myself and only do what actually makes me happy. Right now, going out with you makes me happy, but I don't know how long that will last, especially since the derby season is ending soon and we're not going to have any more of those amazing fights."

She could see as she said she didn't want the same things as Gianna that she'd hurt her, but she kept going anyway. She had to get it all out, as much as she could, so Gianna would understand. If lack of commitment was going to make Gianna leave, Megan wanted it to happen sooner rather than later. She didn't want Gianna going anywhere—she just didn't want Gianna hurt any more than was necessary.

But at the end of her little speech, Gianna was smirking. "Okay, I can accept all that. You just got out of a bad relationship. You deserve a little more leeway. And I meant what I said. I'm with you until one of us decides we don't want it anymore."

Megan nodded. "Okay. But what's so funny?"

Gianna stepped close again, molding her curves to Megan's body. Megan felt her arousal start to awaken again. "I want," Gianna whispered, "you to let me show you that sex is fun even when we haven't been fighting."

Megan's throat was dry. She licked her lips and nodded.

Then she let Gianna guide her to the bed, lay her back, and climb on top of her, her fingers everywhere, her touch bewitching.

CHAPTER 14

"And she's past one, two, three members of the pack. Will she make it past Jazzy Bell? Yes! Margaret Splatwood is our first lead jammer of this match."

The wind was in Megan's hair, in her eyes, making her vision blur, but she didn't care. She could see where the track was, see where the pack was ahead of her again, and she was skating so fast the announcer's words didn't even catch up with her until she was halfway around the track.

That morning, she'd had another appointment with the doctor, and she'd been declared—if not cured, at least unlikely to re-injure herself or slow her healing by playing roller derby, even with Megan giving the doctor a detailed description of everything she did or might do during games. She was told to avoid falling on her left side if at all possible, to break her fall with her wrist if necessary, but cleared to get back on the track as long as she was careful.

It might have helped that Megan had explained that this would be their last game of the season and she was desperate to get back to skating. And that she'd actually gained five pounds since her first time seeing the doctor.

But the important thing was, she was back on the track, and she was well on her way to bringing Monstrous Regiment to a victory for the end of the season. It didn't make any difference, since the team didn't play any tournaments, but it was always good to end on a high note.

Also, Gianna was in the audience, and Megan didn't want to let her down.

The jam ended with the score 12-3, and Megan collapsed on the bench. She was sweating and her legs were shaking. She might have pushed herself a little too hard for her first jam since her injury, but she couldn't have gone any slower if she'd tried.

Shelly gave her a bottle of water, and she sucked it down gratefully. "Are you doing okay?" Shelly asked quietly in her ear.

Megan bit her lip, wanting to tell Shelly she was fine, but knowing she shouldn't. When she realized that Shelly would probably be able to tell if she was lying, she decided to go with the truth. "I think I pushed myself a little too hard. I'm out of shape. I need a break."

Shelly nodded. "I thought you might. I won't put you back in for a while. Maybe a snack, too?"

Megan shook her head and shrugged. It was nice to be able to shrug. She was still supposed to keep her shoulder immobilized as much as possible, but the pain seemed to be pretty much gone.

She recovered enough to play again in the first half of the game, but she was wearing out. She perked up a little when Gianna brought her a soft pretzel during halftime. She gave Gianna a kiss in thanks, not caring who was looking. Okay, pretending to not care who was looking, but it was better than before.

She played twice again in the second half, but it wasn't nearly as much as she normally would have played. If she'd been a little less tired, she would have been fighting with Shelly, trying to get put back on the track. But she knew she was out of shape. She would work all the harder during the off-season to get back in shape—to get better than she'd been before her injury.

Still, she kept the team up on points, and she screamed with everyone else when they won. They shook hands with the opposing team, then skated into the locker room to change. Megan was exhausted, and changed slowly, thinking about seeing Gianna once she was done. Maybe they would actually go to the afterparty this time.

She laced her sneakers on and stood up with satisfaction, happy to be able to tie and untie laces with both hands now. Everyone else had already left the locker room, so she shouldered her bag and headed back out.

The room was mostly clear, but there was a small group

standing on the track and talking. As soon as Megan came out, Shelly turned around, pointed at her, and called, "Megan! Come here!"

Confused and slightly worried, Megan picked up the pace, walking toward her. She definitely had been cleared to play by her doctor. What could Shelly want?

Shelly, Gayle, Leya, Helen, and Mindy were all standing with a pretty woman in her early thirties, whom Megan didn't recognize. She hoped Shelly wasn't about to try to hook her up with someone else. They all looked really excited.

The woman held out her hand as Megan approached. "Megan? I'm Amelia Madden. I'm on the Rittenhouse Rioters."

Megan's eyes widened as she shook Amelia's hand. "You're Dr. Holtzwomann. I saw you last year in the tournament. You were amazing—it was too bad you guys dropped out so quickly."

Amelia grinned. "Then you're already familiar with it. Great. We're working hard to put together a better team this year, and I've been chosen to talk to local players. I want to invite you to try out for the Sisterly Love All-Stars."

Megan's jaw dropped. They wanted her to try out for an all-star team? To maybe take part in a tournament—a game that meant something, even if it wasn't the official WTFDA championships? She knew she was good enough, she'd just... never thought about it before.

She looked around quickly, taking in the delighted faces of the women around her. "All of us?"

"Not me," Shelly said quickly. "Amelia's invited you, Gayle, Helen, Mindy, and Leya. I'm just here to tell you, as your team captain, I highly advise you to *fucking go for it.*"

Mindy and Megan both laughed. Megan couldn't believe it, and she was startled at a touch on her elbow. "What's—oh, hi, Amelia!"

Gianna had approached, probably wondering what was going on, and was standing next to Megan. Megan looked down at her. "You know each other?"

Gianna shook her head. "I just met her earlier this evening. I'm guessing she's here for the same reason she was at my game."

"That's right," Amelia said with a grin. "I'm going around to all the teams in the city, inviting the top players to try out for the all-stars. I haven't been able to watch a full game in weeks. I'll warn you now, competition is going to be fierce."

"As it should be," Megan said. Then she looked down at Gianna again. "You're trying out?"

"I couldn't pass up the opportunity," Gianna said, her eyes sparkling. "I guess I'll see you there."

"When and where?" Helen asked. "I hope I can make it."

Amelia handed out flyers to each of them (except Gianna, who presumably already had them) with information about the tryouts. "Feel free to show up to cheer on our players even if you're not trying out," she said to Shelly. "And invite the rest of your team, too."

Shelly looked down at the flyer. "Can we heckle them instead of cheering them on?"

Amelia laughed. "Absolutely. We don't want any players who can't handle the pressure. What do you say, will I see you there?"

They all said yes, even Shelly, except Megan. She looked down at the paper, swallowing. It was only two weeks away. "I'm just coming back from an injury," she said. "I'm not really in shape yet."

"Try out anyway," Amelia said, waving away her objection. "You looked great tonight, even out of shape. If nothing else, you'll learn the tryout process for next year, right?"

Megan took a deep breath. She didn't know if she could handle that. In front of all those amazing players, from all over the city—including last year's all-star players like Dr. Holtzwomann—when she wasn't at her best? She wanted to play on the all-star team more than anything, but if she wasn't good enough, she didn't think she could stand the humiliation.

She probably would have stood there in indecision for an hour if Gianna hadn't elbowed her in the side. "Come on, babe. What are you, chicken?"

She looked at Gianna, who was giving her a shit-eating grin. They'd both be trying out, she realized. Maybe they played different roles—but there could only be fourteen women on the team, and if one of them made it, that might just be enough to bump the other one off.

She couldn't think of anything she would like more than to compete against Gianna one more time, for much higher stakes.

"Yeah," she said. "I'll be there."

Two weeks later, the day of the tryouts, Megan was almost regretting her decision.

The tryouts were behind held in a huge, echoing arena, full of women. There must have been hundreds of them there, and dozens of men as well—significant others and family of players, support staff, and just guys who were there to watch the tryouts. Megan and Gianna had registered to try out when they arrived, and Megan had seen a glimpse of the list; there had to be a hundred women on it.

The PA system crackled, and a man's voice boomed over all of them. "Ladies, gentlemen, and folks of other genders! Tryouts for the Sisterly Love All-Stars are about to begin! Please take your seats. Those who are trying out, in this section," a spotlight illuminated a chunk of seats that were blocked off from the others, "by the track. Those who are here to spectate and support, take the rest of the stands. Let's get this started!"

Megan turned, swallowing ineffectually against the lump in her throat, and headed for the chairs for the prospective players. She'd almost forgotten Gianna was there and jumped when she took her hand. But she squeezed it and held on until they reached a pair of empty seats.

They both bent to stash their bags under their seats, as everyone else was doing. When Megan sat back up and glanced to her left, she jumped. "Amelia? I thought you were already on the team."

Amelia turned and grinned at her. "Margaret Splatwood, right? I was last year, but I still have to try out again. The whole point is to make sure we have a better team than last year, and that means replacing every single player if we have to. The ones running the tryouts won't be playing, so I wasn't going to get involved in that."

"I don't think they should replace you no matter what," Megan said. She felt like a little bit of a fangirl and hoped Amelia didn't think she had a crush. She could...

Well, she still hadn't made any kind of commitment with Gianna. But it felt like she had. And they were still holding hands.

"How's your injury?" Amelia asked.

Megan reflexively rolled her shoulders, testing them. They both felt equal, as they had for over a week now—no pain in the injured shoulder, and she wasn't icing it or keeping it in a sling at all anymore. She still worried. "It's fine," she said. "I've been careful with it. I'm just concerned that I'm still out of shape after weeks not playing at full capacity."

She'd been working out hard—twice as hard as usual—since Monstrous Regiment's last game, but it had only been at their last practice, on Thursday, that she'd felt herself able to go at full speed the whole night. She had no trust that her energy and strength would stay that high, especially after having Karen and then Joe yell at her at work the day before.

"Well, you'll have to do a fall during the tryout, so just make sure you don't fall onto your injury and make it worse," Amelia said.

Megan nodded, unsurprised, but Gianna leaned forward. "Hey," she said, talking past Megan in a teasing voice, "aren't you supposed to avoid giving any player an advantage?"

Amelia winked. "I like you. But in seriousness, I don't think knowing what's coming up is going to give you any advantage."

A woman dressed for derby started to roll slowly down the front row of seats, handing something to each player. Megan sat up so she could see a little better past the women in front of her and saw that everyone was getting a little orange ticket, like for a raffle. Before she had time to do more than wonder what they could be for, the announcer's voice boomed out again.

"Players, you are now each receiving a ticket. This will be what divides you into groups for the tryout. Look at the numbers on your ticket when you hear announcements."

Megan received her ticket and looked down at it, letting go of Gianna's hand. Her number was 7192534.

As the last few people were given their tickets, the announcer's voice came again. "If your ticket number starts with a six, put your skates on and line up on the track."

A woman standing on the track in skates lifted her arm

to wave at them. Megan looked down at her ticket. Her number started with a seven, but Amelia was bending down and pulling her skates on.

About a third of the women in their section were moving as well, and they started to roll onto the track, pushing through the rows of seats. They'd seated the players close enough that there were no stairs to contend with, thankfully—Megan knew how to hop down stairs on her skates, but she wouldn't trust herself with it right now.

The woman on the track, accompanied by the one giving out tickets, lined up those who had the right number, in groups of six on the track with a good distance between them. Then they stepped off the track and one blew a whistle. The prospective players started to skate.

It seemed to be a simple speed test at this point. Megan could easily pick out the fastest ones—Leya Out was one of them, and Amelia definitely was. As they skated, the woman who'd given out the tickets came back over and told them to start getting ready if their numbers started with a seven. Megan took a deep breath and bent down for her skating bag.

Gianna took her hand and squeezed it. "You'll do great at this phase."

Megan grinned at her. "I know. What's your number?"

"Eight. Just like me." Gianna patted her own hip.

Megan leaned over and kissed her. "Don't be silly. You're a clear ten."

She got her skates on, then followed the small crowd

to the track. The women in charge had the sevens enter the track one way while the sixes left a different way. They were all being sent back to their seats; either this test hadn't allowed them to eliminate the slowest, or they were just waiting to cut down the numbers.

Megan remembered being shouted at by her bosses. She remembered that Gianna was in the audience, watching her. When the whistle was blown for them to start, she put on such a burst of speed that she broke through the line in front of her.

She got a raised eyebrow when they had finished their laps around the track and were being sent back to their seats, and she wondered if she'd been showing off too much. More importantly, she hoped she hadn't just been a total idiot and screwed herself over by using too much energy at the beginning of the tryout.

By the time she got back to her seat, Gianna was already on the track. Megan watched, biting her lip. Gianna wasn't among the fastest, but she wasn't among the slowest, either. She was steady and solid. And smart enough not to show off.

Next they called people by the second number on their tickets, smaller groups this time, ten or twelve in a bunch. They set up an obstacle course of traffic cones on one side of the track and, on the other side, a row of tightly-spaced cones followed by a small stack of gym mats. Megan could see the purpose of this; the skaters would have to show

how quickly they could turn to avoid the cones and how well they could jump on the other side.

She was in the last group this time, so she got to watch Gianna, Amelia, and the few others she knew run the obstacle course. They all acquitted themselves well, though Gianna landed heavily after the long jump and almost lost her balance. Megan found herself biting her lip again and crossing her fingers.

She should be feeling competitive. She should be wanting Gianna to lose out, for a bigger chance that there was space for her. But she couldn't.

Megan practically flew through the obstacle course—it was no problem at all. The girl behind her, on the other hand, didn't turn fast enough and knocked over several cones. When Megan slowed down to make the jump, she realized there were two other women and a man on this side of the track, watching them skate.

Finally, there was one more round, in which they had to jump the cones and the mats again, but this time fall and get up without losing too much speed or, of course, injuring themselves. Megan knew she did well there, too. It was easy to fall and roll right back up again, even on skates, if you did it correctly, and she absolutely knew how. She just had to make sure to fall on her right side.

Now the announcer told them to take a ten-minute break, have a drink and a snack, while the judges conferred. The two women who'd been working with them crossed the track. Of course, if they were going to talk, it would be out of earshot of the players.

Megan got out her water bottle and a bag of peanuts. She drank a little, but she wasn't hungry yet. "It's easy so far," she commented to Gianna.

Gianna grimaced. "It is pretty easy, but it makes me wonder how picky they're being."

"They can't disqualify you based on one little wobble," Megan said, but she was suddenly unsure. The judges had to cut the numbers down somehow, didn't they? Maybe they were only choosing those who were perfect skaters. It didn't really make sense, since people might skate better or worse on one specific day, but they'd already invited only those who were really good players to try out.

A few people got up and moved around, and some others came down from the stands to take advantage of the break—Megan saw Shelly talking to Gayle—but most people stayed where they were, probably just as anxious as Megan was.

Finally, the woman who'd given them their tickets came back, holding a paper list. She started to read off names—derby names. It included Dr. Holtzwomann, Margaret Splatwood, and Mountain Bruise. But what did the names mean? Who were they choosing?

She looked up from the paper and her eyes sparkled wickedly. Megan knew she was enjoying the tension. "If I've called your name," she said, letting the pause drag on far too long, "congratulations, you're being subjected to more torture. If I haven't called your name, you're out. You can go home, or stay and heckle, whatever you want, but get your skates off."

Megan let out a long breath and, without looking, grabbed for Gianna's hand. Gianna squeezed hard. They'd both made it to the next round.

She wracked her brain, trying to remember what other names she recognized from the list. There had been a few from Gianna's team, and a few she thought belonged to other teams she'd played against. Leya and Gayle were on to the next round, too. She hadn't heard Jane the Ripper, so Helen was out, but she wasn't sure about Mindy. Gianna's pirates, though, the sisters—they were still in, too.

Now, occurring to her for the first time, she wondered what it would be like if she had to learn to skate with someone from Rolling in the Streets. She knew she could do it, but she didn't know if she could ever like it. She'd invested too much in competing with them.

Shelly always told her she was too competitive.

Around her, other women were grumbling, swearing, getting their skates off and packing up. One or two were even crying. Megan felt bad for them, but she hoped it would just teach them to work harder next year.

As they drifted off, the woman with the paper was counting. Finally, she looked up. "Okay, those of you who are still going. I'm going to organize you into scrimmages. If your ticket ends with an even number, to my right. If your ticket ends with an odd number, to my left."

They all got up and slowly skated into their groups. Megan found Leya and Mindy—good, she was still in—on her side. They grinned at each other. Megan looked over the group, but found it too many to count quickly, so probably more than a single derby team.

The woman in charge counted the groups. "Okay, odd numbers, there's too many of you. I'll switch two of you to the even side. Let's see..."

Megan saw Gayle over there. She crossed her fingers. If everyone left from Monstrous Regiment was on the same side, they would be amazing.

The woman pointed. "You and you. Mountain Bruise and Smartie Hotpants. Other side."

Megan's eyes widened. She had no idea how to react as Gianna, smirking at her, skated over to join them. She was closely followed by another woman, but Megan didn't give her a second glance.

Was she going to have to skate on the same team as Gianna? They still might get split apart. The groups were too big for one team.

But having seen the first group sent home, it was beginning to seem more real that Megan could actually become part of the all-star team. And if she could, then Gianna could too. Could they even play together? What would that do to their relationship? Megan felt her palms start to sweat.

"Okay. Five, five, five. Five, five, five." Quickly, the woman split them into groups of five—the maximum that could be on the track per team. She moved too fast for Megan to react and try to choose her team, but to her relief, Gianna ended up on a different team, with Mindy. She and Leya were the only ones in their group. Amelia was on the other side, with the pirate sisters; were they going to have to play against them?

"We want to see different play styles, so each track group is going to play a jam against the two other teams from your side," the woman announced. Megan felt her heart start to beat faster.

"Introduce yourselves in your track groups," the woman continued, "so you'll recognize each other when you get there. And pick two jammers and two alternates, because I don't want the same jammer both times. Okay? You have five minutes."

Megan and Leya quickly introduced themselves to the three other women on their track group. Megan did her best to focus on them so she would know who they were, but her eyes kept drifting over to Gianna, who was talking with her arms, as usual.

She was gratified when Leya put her forward as one of the jammers. It wasn't too hard in their small group to decide who would be the first and second jammer and alternate. Now all they had to do was wait to play.

Two of the groups from the odd-number side went first. It was almost as fun to watch them as it was to play herself—they were really good, and Megan found herself cheering as much as the rest of the crowd in the stands. She had no idea how the judges were going to pick just fourteen women to be on the all-star team. Other than Gayle, who never let the opposing jammer through, and was obviously a shoo-in.

They went next; Megan had been selected as the second jammer, so this time she had to play blocker, against a group of women she didn't know. It was strange playing as blocker and she let the other jammer past almost immediately. She swore under her breath at herself. She should have let Shelly put her in as a blocker more often. Sometimes they practiced the other roles, but she had clearly not done enough.

She did better the next time the jammers reached the pack, though she almost blocked her own jammer that time, and almost forgot not to use her elbows. As they finished the jam and skated back to their seats, her stomach twisted. She might have blown her chances.

The other side played again, then the two other groups from their side. Megan watched carefully and couldn't find a single fault with Gianna's skating. Mindy, however, seemed a little slow. Megan just had to hope she was still good enough.

After the last combination from the other side, it was finally Megan's team's turn—playing against Gianna's team. Megan felt herself sweating again, her heart pounding. Playing against Mindy was going to be strange. But playing against Gianna again was going to be amazing.

She stretched her shoulders as they skated into place, she and the opposing jammer coming to a comfortable stop next to each other. It still didn't hurt. She just had to be careful with her energy levels. She could almost let loose now, but she didn't want to collapse when the jam was over.

The whistle blew, and she took off, leaving the opposing jammer in her dust. She slammed into a block from the other team with such force that they were both thrown off the track, and she had to skate back in before the pack left her behind. She almost pushed aside another player, but realized at the last minute that she was on her side—the same person she'd almost blocked last time.

She got a little speed going again, and then Gianna was in her way, blocking her with that magnificent ass. And once again, Megan bounced right off it, her skates going backward and almost out of control.

But not quite. She skated around another blocker, and she bounced off Gianna again. This time she felt fingers on her thigh and she knew Gianna was doing it on purpose.

On her third try, she made it past Gianna, just brushing against her sweaty, silken skin. She gave Gianna a grin as she skated away, skipping past the rest of the pack. If one of them was going to win a place on this team, it would be Megan.

She whipped around the track and made it to the blockers again, with the other team's jammer working to catch her. She caught up while Megan was entangled, almost passing her as Gianna pushed Megan aside with one hip. But Leya and another blocker made a wall with Megan, and they pushed her through, just beating the other blocker.

The jam ended far too soon. Megan was sweaty and panting, but she wasn't falling over. She was just wet. Everywhere.

The important thing was, they'd won. Even if she didn't make it onto the team, she had that to remember.

The tired teams went back to their seats and waited for the judges to confer again. This time, the woman came back with a grin for all of them. "That was awesome. This is going to be a really hard decision, and thank you for that. We have all of your email addresses from when you registered, so you're going to get an email with who is on the team. That should be within the next week. We'll also let those of you who are on the team know when and where practices will be. And those of you who don't make it—definitely come and try out next year."

"A round of applause for our amazing skaters!" the announcer's voice said, and the stands burst into applause and cheers. After a moment, Megan, Gianna, and the others who had been trying out joined in.

Megan couldn't get too enthusiastic about cheering on the other players, though. And it seemed Gianna had the same idea as she did. Gianna grabbed her wrist, pulled her ear close to her mouth, and whispered, "Race you to the car."

It was a tie.

They probably wouldn't have made it past the car if the parking lot hadn't been so crowded. As it was, Gianna peeled out of the lot before anyone else, cutting off another car and making a few pedestrians nervous. "Shoulder still okay?" she asked with a grin.

"It's fine," Megan said, laughing, half-breathless. She didn't know if she actually had enough energy for sex with Gianna now, but she was sure as hell going to try.

They parked near Megan's apartment and held hands tightly as they walked to the door. "Race you upstairs," Gianna said once Megan had opened the door to the stairs, and jumped past the first step on her way up.

"Not fair," Megan protested, hurrying to catch up with her. "The stairwell is too narrow. I can't get past you." She was pressed up against Gianna's ass, which was delightful, but she wanted to win.

"Can't win all the time," Gianna tossed over her shoulder. Megan tried to climb up onto the handrail and over her, just to prove her wrong, but the wood creaked under her weight and she decided not to risk another injury. Not now, when she had a chance of getting onto the all-star team.

Anyway, Gianna couldn't get into the apartment without her. When Gianna made it to the second-floor landing and turned around, Megan pushed her against the door and kissed her, their sweaty bodies melding together in the small space.

"Ex*cuse* me," came a voice from above them. They separated their faces and looked up. Megan's upstairs neighbor, the man with the wife and baby, was standing above them, glaring down his nose at them.

Megan snort-laughed and reached into her bag for her keys. Gianna was shaking with silent laughter. It was extremely hard to find her keys with all of Gianna's jiggly parts rubbing against her that way.

Eventually, though, she managed to unlock the door, and they tumbled inside. The man's footsteps receded down the stairs—Megan was sure he was walking more loudly than necessary. She didn't care.

She retrieved her keys and locked the door behind her, and then she and Gianna were undressing, their lips snatching at each other as they pulled at their clothes.

They raced to the bedroom, and Megan pushed Gianna onto the bed, her hand between her ample thighs. She found Gianna's center, as slick and hot as she knew hers was, and thrust one, then two, then three fingers inside. Gianna screamed and clenched around her, her hands grabbing for the bedsheets.

"Don't stop," she groaned.

Megan took that as a suggestion to go faster, curling her fingers inside Gianna, pressing her more and more full. At the same time, her other hand roamed over Gianna's body, stroking her fleshy curves, everywhere she could reach. And that was a lot, because Gianna was so short.

When Gianna started to pant, Megan added her thumb, pressing it and rubbing against Gianna's clit, mindful of where to press so it would feel good and not hurt. She closed her other hand around Gianna's breast, fingers dimpling the soft flesh.

"C'mon, baby," she encouraged her. Touching her felt so good, she wanted Gianna to feel the same.

Gianna laughed, but soon that laugh turned into a scream of pleasure. Her muscles contracted tightly around Megan's fingers. Megan grinned with triumph.

When Gianna was relaxed again, she lazily raised her arms and pulled Megan close, on top of her on the bed. "What was that?" she murmured.

"What do you mean?" Megan asked. "I figured you would recognize an orgasm when you felt one."

Gianna snorted a quiet laugh. "You called me 'baby.' Usually you don't call me anything. I'm the one that calls you 'babe.'"

"That's true." Megan shook her head. She hadn't thought about it when she'd said it. "I don't think it meant anything. It was just encouragement. And clearly it worked."

"Mm." Gianna pulled Megan closer for a kiss. Megan wanted to lose herself in those soft lips as she did so often, but now she was wondering if she'd meant what she thought she meant, her mind running down confused pathways. Did calling Gianna by a pet name mean she was getting more invested in this relationship? Was that safe? What was this relationship, anyway?

"Hey." Gianna pulled apart, shifting onto her side on the bed, so that Megan also lay sideways, looking at her. "I'm sorry, I didn't mean to make you worry or anything."

"I'm not worrying," Megan said, but it wasn't entirely

true, and from Gianna's raised eyebrows, she didn't think Gianna believed her.

"It's just a term." Gianna smoothed some of Megan's hair back from her face. "But you didn't, uh..."

Megan suddenly realized what Gianna was worried about. Or she hoped she understood. "No, I never called Cari 'baby,' at least not regularly. She didn't like pet names. She called me Meggie."

Gianna smiled, the worry clearing off her face. "Not calling you Meggie. Got it, babe." Her voice dropped, going husky, when she said 'babe,' and Megan shivered all over.

Gianna drew her close again, rolling on top of her, those delicious curves sliding against Megan's sticky, damp skin. She'd forgotten how turned on the tryouts had gotten her, but now her body remembered all over again.

Gianna's hands cupped her breasts, and her mouth followed, sucking Megan's nipples into her mouth one at a time until she was keening, her whole world shrinking to the sharp pleasure in her breasts and the wet heat between her thighs. Then Gianna's hand was there, too, slipping through the slickness to find her center.

Megan spread her thighs, a reaction almost out of the control of her mind, and Gianna slid down between them. Her warm lips and supple tongue were on Megan and inside her, and it wasn't long before Megan, too, was screaming, pleasure exploding all through her body so that she could hardly catch her breath.

Gianna climbed back onto the bed and cuddled against

her, even though they were both sticky with sweat. As Megan tried to get her breath back, Gianna asked, "So how likely do you think it is that either of us made it onto the team?"

Megan couldn't help laughing, though her lungs were exhausted. "Probably not very. There were too many other amazing skaters out there."

"So we didn't need to worry too much about competing with each other."

"No." Megan turned her head and kissed Gianna. "But it sure was fun, wasn't it?"

Gianna put her hand on Megan's waist and tugged her just a tiny bit closer. "It was."

CHAPTER 15

A week after the tryouts, Gianna and Megan had spent the morning in the gym, and were now exhausted, lying around and stuffing themselves full of take out. They were both fully aware that they were just killing time so they didn't spend too much time worrying about the tryouts.

"You done?" Gianna asked Megan, patting her knee.

Megan burped, surprising herself and making them both laugh. "Yeah, I guess so." She felt pretty full—in fact, she didn't think she could eat another bite, tasty as the French food was. It was even hard to imagine getting up from the couch, where they were both so comfortable.

"All right." Gianna heaved herself up from the couch and grabbed both of their food containers from the table.

"You don't have to do that," Megan protested, somehow finding the strength to stand up. She followed Gianna into the kitchen, where she was scraping the leftover food into a Tupperware. "I was going to do that."

Gianna grinned at her. "Well, I win again."

"It's not about winning," Megan huffed, rolling her eyes. "I thought I was the competitive one here."

Gianna gave her a quick kiss on the lips before turning to put her container in the fridge. "I only compete with you because I know how much it turns you on."

Megan was about to make a joke about Gianna trying to seduce her, but it wouldn't have been a very good joke, and anyway, she was interrupted by a trill coming from Gianna's back pocket. Gianna wrinkled her nose as she closed the fridge, then pulled her phone out of her pocket and looked at the screen.

There was a pause.

Gianna's eyes widened as she stared at her phone. "Babe, check your phone."

"What?" Megan took her phone out of her dress pocket and looked at the lock screen. "I don't have any notifications."

"Email."

"Okay... should I be worried?" Megan unlocked her phone and opened the email app—she didn't use it much, since most of the people she talked to would rather text.

"Just trust me." But Gianna was still just staring at her phone, the expression on her face unreadable, so Megan didn't know what to expect.

But she did trust her.

Her email seemed to take forever to load. But when it did, the one at the top had the subject line "SISTERLY LOVE ALL-STARS." Megan grinned and opened the email. She hoped Gayle had made it onto the team—in fact, she was almost sure of it.

She didn't expect the first names she saw, right there in the middle of the list, to be Margaret Splatwood and Mountain Bruise.

She gaped at the list, her knuckles turning white from how tightly she was holding her phone. "We both made it?"

"Looks like it," Gianna said.

Megan scrolled up and down, trying to get a sense of the rest of the email, but all she could comprehend was that numbered list of fourteen names. Sir Blocksalot was on it, too, of course, and Leya Out, and a few other names she recognized—Amelia and the pirate sisters.

But there were their names. Right in the middle of the list. Both of them. Together.

She dropped her phone onto the counter and threw her arms around Gianna, jubilant. "You're amazing!"

Gianna laughed, shoving her phone into her pocket so she could hug Megan back. "*You're* amazing."

Megan kissed Gianna, unwilling to hold back in her excitement, wanting those hot lips against hers. But almost before Gianna could start to kiss her back, she pulled away, a feeling like a lead weight dropping into her stomach. "Crap."

Gianna frowned. "What's wrong, babe?"

“We can’t do this.” Her heart was hammering, slamming in her chest.

“You’re right, I can think of much better ways to celebrate.” Gianna grabbed Megan’s ass.

Megan shook her head. “I don’t think we can... I don’t think we should.”

“Since when are you all moral about having sex with me?” Gianna raised her eyebrows, but she let go of Megan.

“Not if we’re going to be on the same team,” Megan said. She put her elbows on the counter and her chin in her hands. She wasn’t sure how to explain her thoughts to Gianna without it sounding like an insult. But she knew that they couldn’t work together and sleep together.

Besides, Gianna was right about how much she liked competition. What had brought them together but that? She didn’t know if the spark would be there without it.

Gianna would argue with her if she said that, so she had to come up with another way to explain her feelings.

Gianna sighed and leaned her hip against the cabinet. “You really think the Sisterly Love All-Stars are going to have a problem with two team members dating? I bet it happens all the time.”

“I don’t know if it does. No one on my team is dating. Is anyone on yours?”

“Well, no. But we do have a pair of sisters. And they’re on the team, too.”

“I know.” Megan shifted her position so she was leaning against the counter, facing Gianna, her arms crossed over her middle. "But I think if we're all over each other all the time—as we tend to be—then that's going to mess with the team dynamics."

"So we just have to leave each other alone while we're at practice," Gianna said, then frowned. "Okay, I kind of see what you mean."

"It'll be hard for me to put up barriers between practice time and not-practice time, and I think we'll be with the team a lot anyway," Megan said. "It was weird enough at work. And Gayle and Leya already know we're dating, of course."

"Is Leya really her real name?"

"I don't know. But don't get off topic." Megan smiled. "I don't think it'll be too big of a deal. We'll see each other almost every day anyway."

"You got that right," Gianna said, pulling out her phone again. "Did you see that practice schedule?"

"No, not really. It was hard to get past both of us being on the team." Megan looked over at Gianna's phone and saw that the first five practices were already scheduled for the next week—the first one Sunday morning.

Megan groaned. "There go all my lazy, relaxed Sundays that I love so much."

"Complain, complain," Gianna said. "I'm going to have even less time to squeeze in class prep and homework grading."

"It's worth it, though," Megan said.

"Yeah, b—Megan. It's worth it."

Amelia practically met Megan at the door for the first practice of the Sisterly Love All-Stars. She held her hand up for a high-five. "I knew you'd be on the team! You were amazing at tryouts. I'm so excited to skate with you."

Megan grinned. "Me, too." There was an irrepressible thrill bubbling up in her chest at the thought of playing with the All-Stars. She didn't know if she'd be able to slow herself down once she was on skates.

Amelia looked around. "Where's Gianna?"

"Um, I don't know. We came separately." Megan's heart sank a little bit (though it couldn't go very far—she was too excited). If Amelia thought they were always together, what would everyone else be expecting?

But Amelia had been next to them at the tryouts, and she'd seen them holding hands and kissing. No one else would have seen the same things.

Anyway, Amelia clearly didn't think that it was terribly strange that they hadn't arrived together. She just showed Megan where the locker room was and told her they were having a meeting to talk before the actual practice started, so she should just stow her bag. Megan was impatient to get into her skates, but she did what she was told.

When she returned, she saw that Gayle was just arriving, and they high-fived. "I'm so glad someone else from our team made it," Gayle said. "I really thought Mindy would be on, but I guess she wasn't quite at our level."

Megan shrugged. "I was disappointed, too, but I guess they had to find people to cut. It's half luck as much as anything else that we made it. Helen didn't even get to the second round. But Leya's on this team, too, remember?"

Gayle laughed, looking back over her shoulder. "You're right. I sort of forgot about her, she's so quiet. But she's a good choice, too. I guess I just wish we could transplant Monstrous Regiment right into the all-star team." She grinned.

"Yeah," Megan said, grinning back. "It's going to be weird having to learn to play with a different team."

"That's why we're having so many practices," Amelia said, walking up to them with two tall women by her side. "We all have to meet each other and get used to working together. This is Margaret Splatwood and Sir Blocksalot, and this is Meana Murray and Pins'n'Needles."

Megan shook their hands. "Megan. I think I know you. Didn't my team beat yours a few weeks ago?"

Pins'n'Needles laughed, but Amelia interrupted before she could say anything. "No competitiveness. Not with each other. Remember, we're the Sisterly Love All-Stars now, and we're going to crush the teams from other cities."

Megan swallowed. "Right. No competitiveness." Of course, Gianna happened to take that moment to walk in, wave at them, and head over.

Megan let Amelia take the lead, making the introductions

again. Gayle gave Megan an odd look out of the corner of her eye, but she steadfastly ignored it. Now she really regretted letting her team know that she and Gianna were seeing each other. This was not a situation she'd envisioned in that burst of confidence.

Confidence was only for the derby track. She ought to remember that.

The rest of the team soon arrived, and then they were sitting together in the bleachers again. Their chat before practice turned out to be the two women who had run the practice—Kendall and Faith, their new coaches—giving them a pep talk and making sure everyone had met everyone else. Then they sent them back to the locker room to change and start skating laps.

Despite the encouragement to be competitive with other teams and not within the team, the laps soon turned into a race. Megan quickly pulled ahead of everyone except Amelia; the two of them were neck-and-neck, one in front then the other, for several laps. But first Megan fell behind so that Amelia was ahead of her for a whole lap, and then others started to pace her: Meana Murray, then Kiss With a Fist, then Gayle. Megan finally gave up on catching up again and slowed down when she realized her lungs were burning. She might be recovered from her injury, but she still wasn't in the shape she'd like to be.

The coaches surprised her when they had the group stop and told them how long they'd been skating laps: ten minutes, longer than anyone would skate in a match without breaks. They said that the team would be working on stamina, but since it wasn't the top skill in roller derby, they had to work on speed, too.

There was a one-minute water break, and then they were skating laps again. Ten more minutes of regular laps, another break, and then laps with obstacles at intervals that they had to either skate around or jump.

It would have been grueling if Megan didn't love skating so much—just the same thing over and over again. The real fight of roller derby was missing, but she figured they would get there.

During the last set of laps, she and Gianna found themselves next to each other, keeping pace with one another. The backs of their hands touched. Megan wondered whether Gianna had caught up with her on purpose, then wondered whether *she* was the one who had done it on purpose. Either way, it was a lot of fun.

They all hugged it out at the end of the practice—none of them cared how sweaty they were, since all, except Kendall and Faith, were equally drenched—and Megan thought she might be hugging Gianna a little more often than anyone else. But it wasn't too bad. It wasn't like she was longing for Gianna's touch every second.

All right, so she was absolutely longing for Gianna's touch. But she could handle it. No one else seemed to notice her lustful thoughts.

Gayle invited a bunch of people to go with her for burgers afterward, and Megan agreed enthusiastically, but then wished she hadn't when Gianna declined. "I have lesson plans to write," she said, waving goodbye to everyone.

Megan took a deep breath and turned back to face her locker so she would have a moment to compose herself. It was a good thing that they wouldn't be going out together after practice, she reminded herself. They had to act like two ordinary players. They could handle being apart for a while.

CHAPTER 16

After nearly a month of intense, almost-daily practice, the championship tournament was beginning. And Megan believed they were ready.

She wasn't sure if she, personally, was ready. She and Gianna hadn't seen each other outside of practice the entire time, which felt strange, even though they hadn't been dating all that long. At the same time, work was quiet—a trampoline park was a lot less popular in fall and winter than summer—and yet somehow more stressful than ever. Megan had been glad for the extra practice to work off her anger and frustration.

But the team knew how to work together, and they were all amazing players. Megan believed they would win the championship.

She had to believe it. If all that work had been for

nothing, she didn't know what she was going to do with her life.

They were up in New York State for the tournament weekend, but the entire team—Monstrous Regiment and Rolling in the Streets as well, plus most of the other derby teams in the city—had turned up to watch them play and cheer for them. Several other matches were being played the same day, but Megan didn't watch them; she didn't want to know who might be their opponents tomorrow in the second round.

And she knew they would get to the second round.

So she waited impatiently for their turn, the third match, and then waited impatiently again for her turn to play. Kiss With a Fist—Janine—was the jammer in the first jam, and she was amazing, but Megan wanted to be the one on the track.

At the end of the first jam, the Sisterly Love All-Stars were up by just one point, and that was only because Janine had ended the jam a few seconds early, before their opponent could get past Grace O'Malley. After the short break between jams, it was finally Megan's turn.

She skated onto the track to take her spot, exchanging nods with her opponent, who was practically anonymous under her helmet. Then the whistle blew, and they were skating.

As Megan moved with singleminded intensity toward the pack, as she saw the blockers get bigger in her sight, she had a momentary, ridiculous desire to slam herself into

Gianna's body and bounce off, just like old times. It was so strong that she almost felt her skates turning.

But they were on the same team now. It wasn't as fun as competing, but she knew how to do this. Instead of bouncing off, she caught Gianna's arm in hers, and they used each other's momentum to pull her past two of the opposing team's blockers. The other team seemed surprised, like they hadn't even realized she was there.

She and Gianna got separated after that as she struggled her way through the pack, but that was okay. She and the other blockers could get her through this. She made lead jammer, passing the pack, and then she was off again, with so much speed she could hardly comprehend the noise of the crowd over the wind in her ears.

But she could still hear the cheers.

She doubled the score in that jam, pulling them way ahead of the other team, but she knew she needed a break after that much intense skating and fighting. Amelia was the jammer next, and she almost doubled the score again. Megan was screaming for her so loudly she was hoarse.

The match was dizzying in its intensity, more than any match Megan had ever been in before. Of course, she'd never been in an all-star game before. The level of play was even higher than usual, and the crowd was the biggest she'd seen in her life.

They all scarfed down snacks and water during the halftime break, then screamed at each other to psych themselves up for the second half. Their coaches were doing the same, high-fiving them all over the place, telling them they were amazing and they would win this. Megan didn't need the encouragement, but it was still nice to hear.

The second half was a blur, at least when she was on the track, with brief, beautiful moments that stood out in her memory. Sliding under Gayle's legs to pass two blockers. Grabbing hands with Chelsea to spin them both around, knocking the other jammer off her path and getting Megan ahead. Sandwiching beautifully between Gianna and Leya, getting past the entire opposing team before any of them realized that there was a jammer between the two blockers.

And then the announcer was saying their names. And he was telling the crowd that they'd won.

Megan started screaming, jumping up and down, and shaking Gayle and Gianna by the shoulders. They were both gaping, just staring into space, as though they couldn't actually believe their team had won.

Megan believed it. Why not? They were the best.

They did a victory lap around the track, lights shining on them, the crowd screaming and cheering. Then they escaped into their locker room, away from the noise.

The coaches pulled them all into a group hug. "Sisterly Love" wasn't as easy to chant as "Monsters," but they did it anyway, and none of them seemed to mind. Megan certainly didn't. She was too happy.

They couldn't seem to calm down. Then Faith shouted, "Okay, guys, let's party, and tomorrow we're going to win it all over again, right?"

The screams were deafening. Megan wasn't sure if she'd be able to hear or speak after that. And then she and Gianna were holding hands and cheering for each other, and then they were closer together, and then their lips were on each other.

Gianna's body was just as soft and lush as it had always been, her lips and tongue hot and demanding, but no more demanding than Megan's own. She was grabbing her, holding her tight, pressing their lips together so hard she almost had difficulty breathing.

Then her legs wobbled under her, and she took a step back—and realized what she was doing.

"Shit," she said breathlessly, sitting down on the bench with a thump. The others were all still screaming and cheering (except Gayle, who seemed to have left the locker room already)—no one seemed to have noticed them making out.

"Oh, damn. I'm sorry," Gianna said, sitting down next to her.

"Don't be," Megan said. She was still a little out of breath. She needed to rest. And drink a lot of water. And maybe some beer.

Gianna shook her head. "You're the one who pointed out that we had to act like friends. I shouldn't have tricked you into that."

Megan raised her eyebrows. Damn, but it was hard to keep from touching Gianna, even now that they'd just remembered what they were doing and pulled apart. "Did you mean to trick me?"

"Uh, no. I just... well, you were there, and I couldn't help myself."

Megan smiled, then looked away quickly. "Yeah, that's about what I was doing. I think we both tricked each other into it, if anything."

"Do you..." Gianna said, but she trailed off without finishing her sentence.

Megan swallowed. She wasn't sure if she wanted to hear the end of that sentence. But she turned to Gianna anyway. "Do I what?"

Gianna shook her head. "Nothing, never mind. Let's get changed and grab showers. There should be plenty of partying tonight, once the fourth game is over."

"Yeah, good point. We have to rest up for that." Megan bent to remove her skates. She was still grateful to be able to get her own damn skates off. When she got up, Gianna had just finished getting her skates off as well, and without thinking, she reached out to help her up.

Gianna took her hand. It was warm, and soft, and her lips were parted just a little, and Megan wanted to...

No. She let go, a little too quickly, so Gianna stumbled. "Sorry," Megan said hastily.

"It's okay," Gianna said, but she wasn't meeting her eyes.

"Hey, if you guys want showers, you should hurry," said Mary, putting her hand on Gianna's shoulder. "I think just about everybody is heading back to the hotel to clean off."

"Right," Gianna said, turning quickly to her locker. "I better be quick about it if I want to get any hot water."

Megan turned to her own locker, deliberately moving a little more slowly than Gianna, so they wouldn't leave together. The team had taken three hotel rooms in the block, and she and Gianna had made sure not to claim spots in the same room—Megan was sharing with Gayle, Leya, Meana Murray, and Pins'n'Needles (Chelsea and Clara, she reminded herself)—but she still didn't want to have to spend too much time imagining Gianna in the shower, the hot water sluicing all the sweat off her curves, her hands scrubbing all those delicious nooks and crannies with soap...

She'd already spent way, way too much time imagining it.

The next day, their second game was not going quite so well.

Megan felt that most of the team had had too much to drink the night before—herself included—and they were dragging a little. Kendall had bought them all sports drinks before the match, so they were rehydrating, but the first half of the match saw them down almost twenty points.

No one was as happy as they'd been the day before (except maybe Gayle, who had been weirdly cheerful the whole weekend). It was still a lot of fun, but Megan was anxious and annoyed. She really shouldn't have had so much beer. It hadn't worked, anyway; the images of Gianna in the shower had not left her head.

That was probably why she hadn't gotten enough sleep last night, too.

Now that they were on their halftime break, she went to the snack bar to get them all water and some carbs and protein, since the snacks Shelly had brought for them had run out. She thought she'd have to use her roller derby skills to push her way through the crowd, but they seemed to make way for her, even though she'd changed out of her skates and only towered over most of the women, rather than every single person.

Did they recognize her from the track? Were they deliberately making way for her because she was a derby girl? That was hard to fathom. And yet she reached the snacks very quickly.

Loaded down with water, peanuts, and chips, she made her way back to her team, only to hear shouting as she approached. She sped up and dumped the drinks and snacks onto a seat, then changed her mind and grabbed the peanuts before turning to see who was fighting.

It turned out to be Gianna and Chelsea, up in each other's faces and screaming. Faith and Kendall were shouting as well, Faith with her hand on Chelsea's shoulder as though she was trying to separate them, though there didn't seem to be any physical altercation going on. Megan couldn't understand what they were saying over the noise of the crowd and of each other.

"Hey!" She shoved a packet of peanuts into each of their hands. "What's going on?"

"Megan! You—" Gianna smiled at her, but instantly dropped her smile, huffing and turning away. "No, forget it. It doesn't matter. We'll just play as hard as we can." She ripped her packet of peanuts open so viciously that a few spilled out onto the floor.

"Don't do that," Megan said. "Of course it matters. I've never seen you get so worked up before. Just explain what's going on."

Gianna got competitive, she knew, but not like this. Not with someone on their team. There'd been a few arguments among the team members during practices, but since they'd been at the tournament, they'd always presented a united front.

Megan glanced over her shoulder at the other team, on the opposite side of the rink. She could barely distinguish their faces at this distance; hopefully, they were far enough away that they hadn't noticed the screaming match. They would only take advantage of it.

"Don't bother," said Chelsea. "It's shit anyway."

"Hey!" Kendall stepped up to her, past Faith, who let go of Chelsea's shoulder to make way. "You do not talk that way about your teammates, all right? You might disagree, and that's fine, but you don't insult each other's ideas and you don't swear."

"But you—"

"I'll have you benched for the rest of the tournament if you don't let up with it. Believe me, we'd rather have a team that doesn't hate each other than a team that wins the tournament. If you two hate each other we'll have to have you both off the team next year, and what'll that do to our chances? Nothing good."

The corner of Chelsea's mouth turned up. "All right."

Faith had somehow palmed Chelsea's packet of peanuts—she handed it back, torn open. "Stick this in your face, girl, you need it."

"Gianna?" Megan said. She hoped that whatever Gianna's idea had been, she would be able to explain it more calmly now that her blood sugar was back on an even keel.

"Are you sure?" Gianna said.

"Yes," Kendall said, folding her arms. "We want to hear it." Megan was glad that someone else was pushing Gianna; she didn't want it to look like she was just standing up for her girlfriend.

Not that they were girlfriends.

Gianna still glanced at her before taking a deep breath and speaking. "I just think that we're all getting a little too crazy. We need to look at what the other team is doing. They're not as cohesive as we are. I haven't seen them work together, two people aiming for the same specific goal, more than twice. If we work together a little more, we can do better."

Kendall was nodding. "Go on."

"My thought is that whoever the jammer and blockers are for each jam, we need to designate two blockers to be the wingmen and two to deal with the rest of the pack. Remember in yesterday's match, when Leya and I got on either side of Megan and just pulled her through the pack? We barely thought of that in time, but we probably could have done it even faster if we'd talked about it ahead of time."

"That's perfect," Faith said. "Do that."

"We did a lot of other stuff like that, too," Megan said. "I mean, when Chelsea and I spun each other around, that wasn't planned—you can't plan a moment like that—but it worked really well, and the other team obviously wasn't expecting it."

"So we decide ahead of time whether you'll pull something like that if you can manage it, and then you're all ready for it to happen," Kendall said. "I like it. This is a good plan."

Chelsea was staring at Gianna as though she'd grown a second head. "No, that makes perfect sense. I can't believe the rest of us didn't think of it. I thought... er..."

"What did you think I was saying?" Gianna asked, eyebrows raised. She put one hand on her hip, the empty peanut packet fluttering; Megan could tell she was feeling better.

Chelsea smiled a half-smile, turning her head partly to the side. "I thought you wanted to say ahead of time that only some people could help the jammer and the other blockers had to ignore her. It didn't make any sense to me, especially when the jam could change at any moment. But I get it now."

"Oh." Gianna's eyes widened and she nodded. "Yeah, uh... sorry. I see how you might think that. It just seemed so obvious at first, I figured everyone would get what I was saying."

Kendall punched Megan lightly in the shoulder (the right shoulder). "Nice one, Splatwood."

"Me? What did I do? It was Gianna's idea."

"You got them calmed down and talking so they could actually hear each other. Specifically, Gianna. Have you ever considered doing a stint as a captain or coach?"

Megan's eyes widened and she shook her head quickly. "No way, I could never do that. I'd get frustrated and just yell. I'm not that good with people."

Gianna grabbed Megan's arm, surprising her; she thought she'd sat down. "That's not true. You're amazing with people. What about at work?"

"That's different. It's my job. I'd get yelled at if I didn't keep everyone happy."

"Hey, that's not cool. What kind of a job do you have where you get yelled at?" Kendall asked.

"She works at a trampoline park," Gianna said. "It's awesome."

"I'm just the receptionist."

"You do everything else, too." Gianna smirked.

"What, this again?" Megan shook her head. "They only have the one employee, and they let me do all the fun parts of the job anyway."

"Yeah, *working with people*." Gianna shook her head. "I'm not trying to convince you to be a team captain or anything, but you just don't really see your own potential. Here." She shoved a packet of peanuts and a bottle of water into Megan's hands. "Get your strength up. The game is starting up again really soon."

CHAPTER 17

They won. They'd won again, the second round, and next week they would be coming back for the third round of the tournament—the final round, which would determine the roller derby championship for the group.

The Sisterly Love All-Stars were going to that.

There'd been plenty of celebrating, but this time Megan and Gianna had managed to keep themselves under control. People seemed more nervous now than they had yesterday—they couldn't believe they were actually going to the final round. Leya had confessed to Megan that she'd never thought they would get that far, that she would have been satisfied with doing her best, even though she figured they would lose in the first round.

Megan couldn't understand that attitude. She had to believe they would win, because otherwise she knew she wouldn't do her best. And if she didn't do her best and they lost, she would blame herself, and then roller derby wouldn't be fun anymore.

Anyway, they *would* win.

But right now, they were on their way home, carpooling for the long drive back. Gianna hadn't brought her car, since it was too small to pack people into; she, Megan, Janine, and Leya were in Kendall's car, which she was driving. The rest of the team were in other cars, all heading back the same way. That was the main reason they hadn't celebrated as much—almost all of them had to go to work in the morning.

Janine was just telling them about her job search; she was a software engineer, looking for something to move up to with better pay than she had now, but she hadn't found it yet. They had all mentioned that they would probably try to make a career out of roller derby if it was possible, but since there was no pro league, there wasn't really a way to do that.

"I'm really as close as you can get, though. I work for a skate shop." Kendall was looking at Megan in the rearview mirror. "You know, Megan, if you're ever looking for a job, I think you'd do really well there. We could use someone to take on a few extra shifts."

Megan smiled and shook her head. "Thanks, but I have a job I like."

"Where people yell at you all the time."

"I work for a trampoline park. How much better of a job can I get?"

"One where people don't yell at you," Kendall said, laughing. "Anyway, do you actually love trampolining?"

"Uh..." Megan tried to think back to the last time she'd been on a trampoline. It had been an amazing, exhilarating day... but she'd been a kid, no more than ten years old. In all the time she'd worked for the trampoline park, she'd never once found the time to actually jump. "No, I guess not. But I love seeing other people get to."

"And at my work, I get to see other derby girls all day, and other people who love skating. I get to help them find the perfect skates that fit, improve their speed and accuracy, and of course some people really geek out over gear. Not everyone is happy all the time, but what job has that?"

"Not mine," Megan admitted. It was hard to believe, but not every customer who came to the trampoline park was entirely happy. Of course, the ones like Gianna and her kindergarten class (who didn't even complain that the bathrooms were broken) more than made up for the others.

"*And* no one yells at me."

"No one?"

"Okay, customers, once in a while. But Grant—he's my boss, the owner—never gets mad, even once when I was starting and I really screwed up. He just said it's the sort of thing that happens to everyone." Kendall looked in the side mirror, changed lanes, and accelerated to pass a truck.

"Do people really yell at you in your job?" Janine asked, hooking her arm around the seat—she was in the front with Kendall—and turning around to face them in the back seat.

"My office kind of sucks, especially with all the layoffs lately, but no one ever gets yelled at."

"Really?" Megan blinked at her in surprise. "It sounds like such a stressful environment. Nobody gets upset?"

"Yeah, but they're professional about it."

"Then why leave?"

"I kind of expect the same thing wherever I go. Right?" She looked at Leya.

"I've never been yelled at in my job," Leya said, but she didn't tell any of them what job that was. Probably not customer service.

"I'm sure you can't say the same thing," Megan said, looking at Gianna. She felt strange asking that, as though she was looking for someone to back her up, but she didn't actually want any of them to have been yelled at in their jobs.

She'd always figured it was just one of those things you put up with.

Gianna laughed, adjusting the way she sat so that she was facing inward a little bit, her hand on the seat between them to brace herself. Her fingers were brushing against Megan's thigh that way, but it was better than their thighs being pressed together. "Of course I've been yelled at in my job. The kids scream at me all the time, and there's always one or two parents in a year who feel the need to yell at me about grades."

"Wait, don't you teach kindergarten?" asked Kendall.

"They still get grades," Gianna said. "And people freak out about them. But you know who has never yelled at me?"

"The principal," Janine said.

Gianna nodded. "Or the school board, or the board of education, or anybody above me. Professionals don't yell at each other. Parents get emotionally invested, so they can overreact, but it's not the same thing. Megan, you get yelled at by customers sometimes, right? But it's not the same thing as when your bosses yell."

Megan nodded slowly. "Well, you're right. But I figured that was because they're the ones who get to fire me if they want to."

"Are you actually scared of getting fired?" Kendall asked.

"Not really," she admitted. "They don't want to do the work of finding someone to replace me."

"I've never seen you at work, but I bet you pull in a lot of business for them," Janine said. "You're really good with people."

"Isn't she?" Gianna said, grinning.

Megan sighed and shook her head. "I'm not, really. It was just—well, I know Gianna pretty well, and I know our blood sugar gets low after all the..." She trailed off, realizing that Janine was frowning, her eyebrows bunched together. "What?"

"I have no idea what you're talking about," Janine said.

"Oh, did you miss the fight?" Gianna asked.

Janine rolled her eyes. "Who'd you fight with this time?"

"Chelsea. It was over tactics. Megan got us to shut up and talk slowly so we could hear each other."

"That was the whole thing during the break today," Kendall said. "We probably wouldn't have won without Gianna's idea to plan how we would work together. Did you really miss the fight?"

"I guess so," Janine said. "I was, uh... well, I'm used to hearing Gianna scream at people during halftime, and they scream back. I just figure the adrenaline overflows a little during games. I mean, that happens to a lot of us."

"It's never been a problem with Rolling in the Streets," Gianna said quickly.

"That's right." Janine nodded. "Otherwise I would make her shut up. I figured this team was the same."

"Then why did you say I'm good with people?" Megan asked. "I'm not fishing for compliments, I swear, I'm just confused." She wasn't sure if she should believe Janine that she'd missed the fight entirely. Who could've ignored Gianna yelling at the top of her lungs, her arms flying through the air around her?

Janine shrugged. "I can't point to anything specific, it's just something I've noticed since we've been on the team together. You can get people to see your way of thinking, get them to calm down when they're upset."

"Exactly," Kendall said. "That's why I was thinking you'd be a good asset to the skate shop. You make people feel at ease—well, maybe not people in general, but people who aren't scared of bright orange hair and a nose piercing."

"I'm not that good at it," Megan said. "I'm—too competitive."

"Well, that might be true," Janine said. "We're all competitive."

"Shelly, my—I mean, Monstrous Regiment's—team captain always says I'm a little too competitive. She says I need to remember that it's derby, not life and death." But she wasn't really thinking of Shelly. She was remembering Cari, and her sister, and wondering why she had never been able to get either of them to do what she wanted, if she was so good with people.

"Shelly does say that," Leya said. "But maybe that's what allowed you to make it onto this team."

"And that's why we're going to win the tournament, am I right?" Janine grinned, holding up her hand. Megan leaned forward to high-five her.

"Have you really never thought of yourself as good with people?" Gianna asked.

"Well, no." Megan looked at her. She didn't want to point out to the whole rest of the car that she and Gianna had been dating, so she chose her words carefully. "I mean, you've seen some of the people I used to hang out with. You know?"

She'd complained to Gianna about Bonnie, and Gianna had definitely heard the whole saga of her and Cari. She hoped Gianna would understand that she was talking about them.

Gianna smiled. "Just because you're good with people

doesn't mean you're perfect with everybody, especially when it comes to bitches like the ones you're talking about. Sometimes, I think, you're kind of overcompensating. They're hard to get along with, so you try even harder and you end up being a doormat. You know?"

Megan stared at her. Gianna just smiled sunnily back.

"I guess so," she finally said. "I never thought about it that way before, but maybe you're right. And then I go the opposite way when it comes to derby."

"Exactly. You can never win with them, so you'll win there."

Megan sat back in the seat and grinned. "Well, hopefully having this revelation isn't going to keep us from winning. Because we're definitely going to win."

The others all cheered, and then she felt movement at her left side, something tickling her palm. Gianna had found her hand and was holding it. Megan took a deep breath. She should pull her hand away, tell Gianna to let go.

But she didn't want to.

As Megan unlocked the door to her apartment, Kendall having dropped her off on the way to the other girls' houses, her phone buzzed. She winced, expecting Bonnie; everyone else she cared about knew where she was today and had probably been there with her.

But when she got inside and looked at her phone, she found a text from Gianna. *We need to talk.*

She sat down on her couch and stared at the text. If she and Gianna hadn't already broken up—not that they were together in the first place—she would have thought that Gianna was about to break up with her. But that was obviously nonsense. What could it be?

What about? she texted back.

The response took long enough to come that she started getting nervous. But Gianna was still in the car with the others—maybe she didn't want to make it obvious that she was texting Megan.

No, this is a convo I want to have in person. Talk after practice?

The coaches had made sure all the members of the Sisterly Love All-Stars understood that they were still going to have practice every single night that week. Megan looked forward to it. Not only did she need the outlet after a long day at work, she knew they couldn't let themselves get complacent in the least. They had to be in the best shape of their lives for the championship game that weekend.

Won't that keep us up late? We both have work in the morning, she texted back.

Don't care, came the reply, quickly this time. *It'll be worth it.*

Megan sighed. She couldn't think of any other excuses. Besides, whatever Gianna wanted to talk about, it couldn't be bad, right? They were getting along well enough, and they were both skating really well. What else mattered?

OK, she texted back. Then, refusing to allow herself to dwell on it, she went to find something to watch that would relax her brain until she was tired enough to sleep.

CHAPTER 18

Practice went really well that night. They were all energized after their two victories that weekend—the only times they stopped talking about it was when they were too out of breath from skating—and no one wanted to slow down or relax. That would look weak in front of the rest of this amazing team.

They also all wanted to win the next weekend. That meant practicing the best so they could be the best.

Megan had worked hard enough that when Gianna caught her arm in the locker room and led her out to her car she only felt a little nervous. She hadn't forgotten that she and Gianna were supposed to talk, of course, but maybe she'd hoped Gianna had.

"Whatever this is," she said, "can't it wait until after the tournament?"

Gianna looked down, her hands pressed together. "I don't think so. It's been hard enough to stand it this past weekend, being so close to you."

Megan's heart jolted in her chest. "Gianna, I thought—"

Gianna held up her hand. "Let's get somewhere we can sit and see each other properly before we talk, all right? Do you want to go to my place or yours? Or maybe somewhere we can sit and get a drink?"

Megan thought of the Zonia Cantina and swallowed hard. Not there. Maybe never there again. "Your place," she said, because she didn't want to have this talk in an intimate setting like her apartment. "As long as you don't mind potentially helping me get home afterward."

"Shit. You're right." Gianna ran her hand over her face. "Your place, then? Just because I don't know how this conversation is going to end, so I'm not sure I'll be up to driving you home."

Megan bit her lip. It wasn't perfect, but she didn't want to end up stuck at Gianna's apartment. Especially if they had a fight, which it sounded like might be in the works.

"Yeah. I guess that's okay."

They got in the car, and Gianna drove to Megan's apartment in silence. Megan didn't want to say anything, because she could only think of one conversation topic, and if Gianna didn't want to start it in the parking lot, Megan was sure she didn't want to start it while she was focusing on driving.

Megan thought her apartment looked small and dingy

in the evening darkness, but at least she had a couch. "You want something to drink? Water, beer?"

"Yeah, water, I guess. Thanks."

Megan poured them each a glass of water while Gianna sat down, then joined her on the couch, trying not to touch her. Now that they were alone, in her apartment—she was afraid that if she touched Gianna's warm skin, she wouldn't be able to help herself.

"You're not running off to join the circus, right?" she said, trying to smile. It was a pretty stupid attempt at a joke. Definitely not up to her usual standards.

"Megan, I love you," Gianna said, her hands holding the water glass very still.

Megan's heart skipped a beat. She stared at Gianna, a lump growing in her throat. She wanted to make a joke, but it would have been even worse than before... and anyway, she knew Gianna meant it.

"Why do we have to talk about that?" she whispered.

"Because there's no reason we shouldn't be together. We can't keep our hands off each other even when we try our hardest, and no one cares. Do you think anyone batted an eye when we made out after Saturday's match?" She put down her glass very carefully.

"They didn't notice," Megan said.

Gianna shook her head. "I know Faith saw us, and I think some of the other players did, too. Besides, all the girls from both our teams knew we used to date. Your team knew, right?"

Megan nodded. If only she'd tried harder to hide it... but she had a lot of regrets in her life, and dwelling on them had never done any good.

Gianna took Megan's hand between both of her own. Megan's heart started beating harder. "One of the things we were both worried about has obviously turned out to be untrue."

"What thing?" Megan's mouth was a little dry; it was hard to get her words out, but she didn't want to pull away from Gianna's hands to get her water.

"That we're only into each other because of the competition. Don't get me wrong, it obviously helped. But it's still hard to keep away from each other when we're working together." Gianna gave Megan a smile, a pale imitation of her usual triumphant grin—but the spark of it was still there.

Megan took a deep breath. "Yeah. You're right about that. But..."

"If it's that you don't feel as strongly about me as I feel about you, I know that, and I'm okay with it. I just want to give it another try."

"I don't know if I can really do that right now. Not when we're so focused on the tournament."

"Didn't you say yesterday that you're too competitive?"

"Yeah, and then you said I act like a doormat."

"I didn't mean it as an insult—"

"I know," Megan said quickly, squeezing Gianna's hand. "But you were right. And with you I've been overcompensating in the opposite direction—I don't want to end up like

I did with Cari, so I'm trying to be in control all the time. And that's not really healthy, either. Not for a serious relationship. I don't think I'm in any place to have any kind of relationship until I work on myself a little more."

Gianna chewed her lower lip. "Okay, I guess that's fair. It hurts, but I can't argue with it."

"I'm sorry," Megan said, wincing. The last thing she wanted to do was hurt Gianna. She knew that was why she had to say this. "It sucks, but I think it would suck a lot worse if we got together, then had a nasty breakup in six months. And if we hated each other—"

"That would really screw up our derby teams," Gianna finished for her, smiling. "You're right."

She leaned forward and kissed Megan on the lips. Megan kissed her back, her heart aching. All she wanted to do was kiss Gianna and keep kissing her, but she knew that wouldn't be fair.

She cared about Gianna too much. Maybe even loved her. With some distance from the sex, she knew it now: she'd rather break Gianna's heart just a little bit now than do the easy thing now and make it harder later on.

Finally Gianna broke away. "Okay, I'd better get home and get some sleep before work. I'll see you tomorrow. Let me know when you're ready to talk again?"

"Yeah," Megan said. "I will."

She didn't know when she would be ready.

She didn't know if she ever would be.

Megan's head ached. She'd had too much coffee to make up for the lack of sleep last night. Of course, "too much" coffee just meant she'd made one stop at Starbucks on her way to work—she didn't normally drink coffee at all, since derby helped her sleep like the dead every night.

Plus, the phone seemed to be ringing constantly today, which was especially unusual since they were normally less busy in the winter and it was now December. Unfortunately, the actual bookings were no more than she would have expected—more than half the people she talked to, even with Megan trying her best to sell the trampoline park, decided not to book that day.

Thankfully, it was now time for her lunch break. She silenced the phone and set the screensaver on her computer. She would probably have to catch up on a few phone messages when she got back, making her afternoon even busier, but right now it was worth it.

Unfortunately, she'd just taken a bite of her sandwich and opened her phone to scroll for mindless entertainment when Karen popped out of the office. "Megan, now that you're off the phone, can you come talk to us for a few minutes?"

Megan swallowed painfully. "Can it wait? I'm on my lunch break." She sounded like she was whining, so she hastily took a drink of water and tried to arrange her face into a respectful expression.

Karen shook her head. "No. We need to talk."

Great. The second time in two days. Was she getting

fired? She took another gulp of her water and followed Karen into the office.

"Hi, Megan," Joe said with a friendly smile. She immediately distrusted his appearance. She also noticed that they didn't offer her a seat—not that there was an extra one to offer her, with just the two desks and one chair for each. What was going on?

She took a deep breath. She had to wait for them to speak first before she freaked out.

"We have a request for you," Joe said. "Karen and I are taking a vacation over Christmas—two weeks on a cruise."

They weren't going to ask her to come along with them, were they? Maybe they were going to ask if she could go the two weeks without pay while they closed the trampoline park. She could handle that, especially over Christmas—she could ask Bonnie and her parents for cash gifts, which they would probably be happy to provide, considering it didn't require any thought.

But, damn, she would have to call people to cancel their reservations or reschedule them. She knew there were some reservations around Christmas, including one the day after. No one would be happy about that.

"Sounds like fun," she managed.

"We'll need you to run the place while we're gone," Karen said. She was leaning against her desk, her hands resting on the edge. So there was an empty chair.

"That means coming in at your regular time, but staying to close the place up at nine, and getting it cleaned up like you usually do," Joe said. "I know you can handle that. You're the best employee we've ever had." He beamed at her.

She stared back at him. Yeah, she was the best employee they'd ever had, because she was the only one. Or maybe just the only one who'd lasted longer than a few months. It was nice to hear that they trusted her with a job this big, but she wasn't sure she wanted it.

"We wanted to let you know now, before you make any plans for the holiday," Karen said. "Of course, we're closed on Christmas, but goodness knows the holiday season isn't limited to just the one day."

"Christmas Eve, too," Megan said.

"What?" Karen leaned forward just a little.

"We're closed Christmas Eve and Christmas Day. The calendar says so."

Karen frowned and looked across at Joe. "That's not what I remember."

Joe frowned and looked at Megan. "Are you sure, Megan?"

"I'm the one who does the scheduling, remember?" she said. "The calendar says we're closed both days."

"Oh, well." He smiled again. "That makes it easier for you, doesn't it?"

"Yeah." She was trying to think. How was she going to deal with this? She'd still be able to see her family for Christmas—assuming they didn't try to make plans for some time that was more convenient than Christmas, at least according to her dad. But the derby girls might want to do something for the holiday, and she might want to see Gianna...

Roller derby.

If she was staying here until closing, she would miss roller derby.

Of course, the tournament was ending this weekend, so she wouldn't be letting down the all-star team. But she would miss a lot of practices, since the Monstrous Regiment never stopped practicing. She would have no outlet for her stress, unless she gave up sleep to take up running or something like that.

She took a deep breath. She could do this. She would have to find a way.

"Okay," she said. "I appreciate your trust in me. How much will I get paid for the overtime? Time-and-a-half?"

Joe looked down and shuffled some papers on his desk. Karen said, "We were hoping you would take on the extra hours as a volunteer. We can't afford to pay extra—not with the cruise."

"But after the cruise, we'll talk about a raise," Joe said. "We're thinking about switching up your hours anyway. You're so good with the customers that it would really be best to have you here during our busiest evening hours."

"Especially after what Joe said to that family last week," Karen said nastily.

"We need you, Megan," Joe finished.

Yes. They needed her. She knew that perfectly well; this place hardly ran without her, especially if that canceled appointment from last week had been because Joe said something rude to a family, which it sounded like it was. She had to stay and do this stuff because otherwise, there would be no one to do it.

It was going to be hard, but that was just what you had to do to keep a job in this economy.

Then she remembered Gianna from two days ago. *Sometimes, I think, you're kind of overcompensating. They're hard to get along with, so you try even harder and you end up being a doormat.*

And Gianna from even longer ago, pointing out that she did everything here. And the other girls in the car on the way back from the tournament, none of whom had ever been yelled at by their bosses.

They probably had never been asked to work unpaid overtime, either.

She took yet another deep breath. She was afraid to say this, but she knew she had to. She couldn't let other people control her life.

She straightened her shoulders, looked Joe in the eyes, and then turned to Karen.

"No," she said.

Karen narrowed her eyes at her. "No?"

"I'm not working any overtime and I'm not changing my schedule to evenings," she said. "I have roller derby practice in the evenings and I'm not willing to give that up. Find someone else to cover that shift if you need it."

It felt surprisingly good to say no. She wanted to keep

going, to shout at them, to tell them that they could do some of the work themselves if it needed to be done and that if they couldn't afford to run their business they couldn't afford to go on a cruise either, but she held her tongue. This was enough.

Karen continued to look pissed, but it was Joe who exploded, standing up and leaning over his desk to wag his finger in Megan's face. "What the fuck, Megan! How dare you refuse this opportunity! You know, this whole place could be yours when we retire, but not if you're going to be so ungrateful! Maybe we will find someone else to do your job, and then where will you be?"

"Joe," Karen said, dropping her arms, "she has the right to choose what she's going to do and not do in her job." Megan hated it when they switched who was good cop and who was bad cop.

"Shut up, Karen. We're her bosses! She doesn't have a choice except to do what we tell her to do!"

"Yes, I do," Megan said. Her heart was pounding. She wanted to step back, but she held her ground. She wouldn't let Joe know that he intimidated her.

Karen crossed the small space to get closer to Joe. "Leave her alone," she whispered. "Just give her time to think about it, and I'm sure—"

"You're not even listening, Karen!" Joe bellowed. "Megan, you'll open and close the park while we're away for Christmas, or we're replacing you."

"Fine." Megan did take a step back this time, but only to

get closer to the door. "But you're not going to have my help finding my replacement. I quit, effective today."

They both turned to face her this time. "You can't!" Karen cried.

"Yes, I can," Megan said. She stepped through the doorway. "I don't need you."

Karen ran after her, but she backed around the desk and Karen stopped, hands dangling at her side. "Megan, please. What do you need? More money? We'll raise your pay. You'll get free tickets for the park."

Megan was gathering up her lunch. She'd eat it outside. She looked at the phone and felt a lurch of guilt; the light blinked with three new messages already, and she wasn't answering any of them. She was leaving the customers to the dubious good nature of Joe and Karen.

"You might want to offer the next person more money," she said calmly. "They're going to have a mess to deal with, and you're going to have a hard time finding someone willing to take on this job."

"Are you threatening me?" Karen hissed.

Megan shook her head. "I'm just leaving. I can't threaten you if you don't have anything that I want."

She did consider threatening them, of course. It would have been really satisfying to start throwing a few punches. But it wasn't worth the risk—not unless they forced her to it. She and Karen stared at each other for a long, silent moment.

In the end, Karen stepped aside and Joe stayed in the office. They let her walk out of there.

CHAPTER 19

Megan was drenched with sweat and sucking desperately on a bottle of sports drink. The coaches had filled their trunks with drinks and snacks this time, and it was a good thing they had: this final, championship match was the toughest game they'd ever played.

It was halftime break, and the scores were actually tied.

The crowd was wild, and Megan felt pretty wild herself, buzzing with energy even though she hadn't had any caffeine that day. During breaks, her eyes kept straying to Gianna, but on the track, she was totally focused.

The only explanation she could come up with for the fact that they weren't winning was that the other team was really, incredibly good.

"All right, folks, let's talk tactics in the few minutes we have left," Faith said, gathering them all together. Megan noticed that Gayle had been talking to Shelly over the barrier that separated them from the audience. She waved at Shelly, who grinned and waved back, but then they were all huddled together, looking at the coaches, and there was no time for anyone else.

"You're all doing really well with the teamwork thing," Faith said, looking at each player in turn. "Gianna's idea is still holding strong."

"But it's not enough," Amelia said. "We don't have teamwork as an advantage over the other guys like we did last week."

"Yeah," Grace said. "They also seem to really know what they're doing and how to work together."

"So we need to come up with something else, if we can," Kendall said. "Gianna, any ideas?"

Gianna blinked in obvious surprise. "Me? No." Megan grinned. She was so cute.

"I keep trying to come up with tricks, and they're all dirty tricks that are going to get somebody suspended," Janine said with a grimace. "It feels like that would be the only way to win."

"Not true," Faith said. "You guys are an amazing team and you can win without any tricks. They're not perfect, right?"

"You're the ones who have been watching the whole match from the outside," Megan said. "Have you found any weaknesses we can exploit?"

Faith grimaced. "To be honest, no. But I don't think

they've found any weaknesses on our side, either. All we have here is two solid derby teams."

"So just be our amazing selves. That's our tactic." Megan grinned.

Gianna caught her eyes and grinned back. "I think that's definitely the best thing we can do."

The whistle blew, signaling that they only had a short time until the second half of the game began. "Okay," Kendall said. "This is it. No fancy tactics, no head games. Just amazing derby."

As they all cheered to pump each other up, Faith shouted over them, "And don't hurt yourselves!"

Megan had that advice in mind as she positioned herself with the other jammer for the first jam. Her heart was pounding. She looked over at the opposing jammer and nodded, adjusting her gloves. The other woman gave her a weak grin.

At least they think we're as much a threat to them as they are to us, was all Megan had time to think before the whistle blew again and they were off.

She managed to get them up by a single point, but then in the next jam they were down to a tied score again. Amelia, in the next jam after that, got them two points ahead, but in the following jam they didn't make any points at all, so the other team was up by seven.

They managed to regain the tie, but for the next few rounds it was up and down again, just a few every time, always so close it would have been impossible for Megan to keep track if it weren't for the announcer. Even with his PA system, it was sometimes hard to hear him—the crowd was cheering so loudly.

Megan was exhilarated. She'd played against really strong opponents before, but (much as she loved Monstrous Regiment) the team she was on had never been so cohesive and so good. This was competition. This was *derby*.

As the penultimate jam wore down, Faith pulled her aside. "Your shoulder, it's in good shape, right?" she whispered urgently. "No pain?"

Megan moved her arm up and down, just to make sure, and nodded. "It's totally fine," she reported. She hadn't felt a twinge since practice for the All-Stars had begun—but she needed to be certain she wasn't lying to her coach.

Faith nodded, her face relaxing slightly. "Good. I'm putting you in for the final jam, if that's okay. It was going to be Janine, but it looks like she has a bit of a strain in her leg, and I'm not putting Amelia in twice in a row. You're going to kill this for us, right, Megan?"

Megan took a deep breath. She used the moment to check over all her systems, to make sure she wasn't having any pain anywhere, that she was ready.

She nodded.

"Great," Faith said, tugging her back to the rest of the team. "Guys, Megan's jammer for the last jam. Get any planning you need in... now."

As she spoke her final word, the whistle blew. They only had thirty seconds to plan. Megan and Gianna locked eyes.

They knew what to do.

The two teams were tied at the beginning of the jam. If they stayed tied, the match would go into overtime. That wasn't a bad thing... but the Sisterly Love All-Stars were dragging, and, if Faith was right (and she usually was), one of their jammers was injured. They needed to end the game, and preferably end it on a win.

That was all that was going through Megan's head as she skated to take her place for the final jam. She had to make lead jammer, and she had to pay attention to the score. If she ended the jam too early, they would have room for another jam in the period, so she had to get her team's score up, keep it up for at least a minute, and end the jam before the other team could get ahead again.

No small task.

This time she didn't look at the opposing jammer while they waited on the line. She didn't want to see the other team as people. She just wanted to win.

As soon as the whistle blew, she exploded off the jammer line, off like a rocket toward the pack of blockers. She didn't look at the other jammer; she didn't want to slow herself down enough to see what was happening.

She found Gianna at the back of the pack. They grabbed each other's hands and pulled together. They didn't hold onto each other; they just skated, shoulder-to-shoulder, forming a wall but not an impenetrable one.

Their opponents could get through them without breaking anything, so they weren't breaking the rules. They were just skating very, very close together, with no space between them. In fact, there was practically negative space between them, the way Megan was pressed against Gianna's cushiony body.

But she wasn't distracted. Not this time. She just had to play.

The two whistle blasts came before she made it through the pack, though, and she swore under her breath. The other jammer had already made lead. Now Megan had to catch up.

As soon as she had gotten through the pack for the first time, she took off skating fast again. She passed the other jammer and reached the pack a few feet ahead of her. She slid past one of the opposing blockers and inwardly cheered. They were up a point!

But she couldn't stop the jam even if she wanted to now. She just had to keep the points up for the rest of the jam, so that the other jammer never had a good place to end it.

She struggled through the pack, assisted by Gianna, Leya, and her other teammates. But it was difficult for them to assist her thoroughly while also blocking the other jammer, and they burst through the pack at the exact same time. They were still tied. They raced around the track, each trying to beat the other to the pack, but neither of them could get any speed on the other.

They hit the pack again. Megan's heart was beating hard. They didn't have much time. She had to get them ahead so they didn't go into overtime. She had to...

They made it through the pack again. They spun their skates faster than ever before. Megan had never gone this fast without worrying that she was going to shoot straight off the track and into the crowd.

They hit the pack and Megan slid through Gianna and Leya, who came together right behind her, blocking the other jammer. Megan didn't have time to look back to see how she was doing. She tucked her elbows in and pushed her way through the pack.

She had never wanted to use her elbows more than she did at this moment, but she could never afford a penalty less.

Often she could see over the heads of the other players, but for this final jam, the opposing team had fielded some really big women. Megan couldn't see past the ones she was trying to get around. All she could do was skate as hard as she could.

And then the woman blocking her was shoved aside by a short, curvy, ballistic missile. Megan grinned with excitement. She made it past the next blocker, and then—

The whistle blew. Four short blasts signaling the end of the jam. Had the other jammer called it?

No, she saw as the pack slowed and cleared, she was right next to Megan, still detangling herself from a blocker. Was it still a tie?

The scores weren't shown anywhere. They spun in slow circles, staring up at the announcer's booth.

"By a single point," the announcer cried, unable to keep

his own excitement out of his voice, "the winner is... The Big Apple Roller Babes!"

The crowd exploded with cheers. The women beside her on the track exploded with cheers. And, amazingly, Megan found herself exploding with cheers, too.

The other jammer held up her hand. Megan high-fived her. The blockers were high-fiving, too, and shaking hands, and then the rest of both teams were pouring onto the track, cheering and hugging and shaking hands over and over again.

Megan couldn't stop laughing. That had been an incredible game. When she found herself face-to-face with the opposing jammer from the last jam again, she wrung the other woman's hand. "That was amazing," she shouted, unsure if she'd even hear her over the noise of the crowd and the teams. "We should do it again sometime."

"Absolutely," the woman shouted back, grinning her head off. "We'll see you next year."

The Sisterly Love All-Stars made their way off the track so the Roller Babes could do their victory lap. Everyone kept cheering and cheering. Megan's throat was getting sore. She and Gianna kept hugging and jumping up and down.

They hadn't won. But they'd lost by a single point.

And somehow, that felt just as amazing.

The entire team slept like the dead that night, even after partying for hours. It was a good thing they'd taken hotel rooms again, because they had no chance of being in good enough shape to drive back the same night. As it was, it took them a few hours and a lot of greasy hotel breakfast and weak hotel coffee to get going.

Megan was glad she didn't drive. No one was going to ask her to, and she didn't have to be entirely awake. She just had to get rested enough for her interview tomorrow.

But she felt oddly alert, despite the pounding headache and the dry mouth. Her mind was clear. For what felt like the first time in years—maybe ever—she knew where she was going and what she was doing.

As Faith pulled her car onto the highway, Megan and a few others riding as passengers, Megan turned to Gianna. "I think you got it wrong."

"Who, me? Never. What did I get wrong?" Gianna flashed her grin at Megan—but it was only a flash, and she bit her lip afterward. Megan's heart lurched as she realized Gianna probably thought she was talking about their relationship.

"About me," she said quickly. "I stood up for myself quitting my job."

Gianna's smile returned. "Yes, you did, and it was awesome."

She'd told all the girls about how she'd quit her job the same evening at roller derby practice—she hadn't been able to hold it back, and they'd all been thrilled for her. Kendall had immediately set her up for an interview at the skate shop where she worked. It was slated for Monday, and would pay a lot more than Megan had been earning at the trampoline park, so she wasn't too nervous about living on her savings in the meantime. Assuming she got the job.

She wasn't feeling all that awesome at the moment.

"It wasn't that awesome," she said. "Just overdue. But my point is, I was being a doormat, but not because I was overcompensating."

Gianna raised her eyebrows. "Do tell."

"It's roller derby where I've been overcompensating," she said. "I've never thought I could stand up for myself. But in derby..."

"You just knock other people down," put in Clara with a laugh.

"Exactly," Megan said, turning to grin at her. "It's the only place where I ever thought I could win. And I thought it was the thing—I mean, it definitely was the thing that gave me the confidence to finally break up with my ex, because that needed to happen. But I didn't really break up with her because I was confident. It's, um, a long story."

"I know what you mean," Gianna said. Of course, she was the only one in the car who knew that Cari had been abusive, and Megan wanted to keep it that way. She wasn't sure if she felt embarrassed about it anymore—she knew it wasn't really her fault—but that didn't mean she wanted to drag out her history in front of everyone, either.

"I had to think about it yesterday, because I felt so good even though we lost."

"You guys played your hearts out," Faith said. "It was

amazing. You should absolutely be proud of how well you did."

"And I am," Megan told her. "I'm proud and I'm thrilled and I'm grateful to you and Kendall and the rest of the team. And especially you, Gianna, because you made me think about things. You made me think about myself."

"And you're feeling good about yourself?" Gianna asked, her voice lower.

Megan nodded. "I guess I always thought that if I didn't win, there wasn't any point. Why should I try? I never could win with my sister, I never could win with my ex, I never could win with work. But—it sounds like a stupid moral to an after-school special, but it's true. I don't have to win, as long as I know I did my best. I did what's right for me."

She put her hand on Gianna's where it lay between them on the seat. Gianna's eyes widened, and she turned her hand slowly over so their palms were facing. She squeezed.

"So," she said, her voice even quieter than before, "you're ready to talk?"

Megan nodded. "I think so."

Gianna got out of the car when Faith pulled up at Megan's apartment, and they both got their bags out of the trunk. "I'm staying here," she told Faith through the window of the car.

Faith raised her eyebrows. "You sure about that?"

"Absolutely," Megan said. Gianna turned slowly to stare at her.

Faith grinned and made an obscene gesture. "Time to celebrate, huh? Have fun, girls." With no more discussion, she drove off, leaving Megan and Gianna on the sidewalk.

"Have I finally succeeded in ridding you of embarrassment?" Gianna asked as she followed Megan up the stairs.

"Don't give yourself too much credit," Megan teased. "You helped me figure out my confidence and doormat issues, but not that one."

"Yeah?" Gianna leaned against the wall as Megan unlocked her apartment door. "So what made you less embarrassed?"

"I decided it was stupid." Megan stepped into the apartment and held the door open for Gianna. "I was really just making excuses." She dropped her bag and turned to lock the door behind them, giving Gianna a moment to put down her own bag.

"You're done with excuses?" Gianna said softly. Megan heard the quiet thump and turned.

"Yeah," she said, and she took Gianna's face in both hands, and she kissed her.

Gianna made a soft noise against her mouth that just made Megan want to kiss her harder, and longer; she backed her up against the couch, their bodies pressing together, and Gianna's arms came around her waist and held her tight.

When they had to break away for a moment for air, Megan let her hands slide down from Gianna's face to her shoulders, and Gianna looked up with a wicked grin.

"I thought you wanted to talk," she said.

"I did. I do. But I had to do that first, so you'd know I was serious."

Gianna's smile faded and she shook her head. "But I don't know that you're serious. We do this all the time, Megan. I'm still willing to wait for you, but not if you're going to toy with me."

"All right." Megan took a deep breath and looked into Gianna's eyes. "I'm not going to toy with you and I'm not going to make you wait."

"Make that a little clearer for me, babe," Gianna said, her gaze steady.

"I want you to be mine, Gianna. I want you to be my girlfriend. I love you."

Gianna gave a little gasp. Megan felt it all through her body. "You mean it?" she whispered.

Megan nodded. Her heart was beating hard, just like it did in roller derby. This was exhilarating and frightening at the same time.

If she didn't win, she would at least know that she'd done what was right for her.

"You get me, Gianna. More than anyone else ever has. I've been scared of ending up with someone like Cari again, but you've proven over and over again that I don't have to be scared of you." She slid her hands down over Gianna's shoulders and down to her waist. "I couldn't promise you anything as long as I wasn't sure I was a whole person. But now I know I am. You helped me figure it out. If you say no, I'll be brokenhearted, but I'll still be me."

"Megan," Gianna whispered. "You know I want this."

Megan smiled. "I just want you to confirm for me that I haven't screwed the whole thing up. I've kind of been a douche to you..."

Gianna lifted her hands to the back of Megan's head and pulled it down. Their lips pressed together, kissing, pulling, biting, hot and wet. After not enough time, Gianna pulled her head away again. "That's to show you I'm serious."

Megan grinned. "Are you serious?"

"I love you," Gianna said. "Want to move into my unnecessarily huge apartment with me?"

"Won't your parents mind? You said they helped you pay for it."

"Babe," Gianna declared, "they are going to absolutely love you. In fact, I want you to meet them this weekend. You up for it?"

"Yes," Megan said, and surprised herself a little bit by how much she meant it. She wanted Gianna in her life entirely—and that meant her family would be part of her life, too. Gianna had mentioned her parents enough and in positive enough terms that Megan was actually excited to meet them.

"And am I going to get to meet your family?"

Megan grimaced. "I'll set something up with my mom,

but it might take me a little longer to get around to my dad and Bonnie. You don't want to meet them if you don't have to."

"Megan. Babe. Sweetheart." Gianna pulled Megan's head down for another kiss. Megan was starting to get lightheaded. "I want everything about you. That means the crappy parts, too. Can I deck your sister when I meet her?"

Megan laughed and shook her head. "She's not so bad anymore. If you ever see Cari in the street, though, she's the one that deserves it."

"Nah," Gianna said. "The best revenge is living well. I'll just show her how happy you are without her."

Megan gave Gianna a squeeze. "I am happy. You know that, right?"

Gianna kissed her again, this time with tongue, a wet heat that went all the way down to Megan's sex. She shivered, all her nerves suddenly on alert.

"Have we talked enough?" Gianna whispered.

Megan nodded, swallowing. "Don't you need to get home? You have work in the morning."

"I'll call out sick. I've been planning ahead for this day."

Megan allowed herself a grin. "You were that sure of me?"

Gianna laughed. "Well, not this specifically. But that's why I've made sure to have lesson plans, so a sub can fill in for me. The kids will be fine. Tonight, all I want is you. And tomorrow I'll drive you to your job interview so your nice outfit won't get messed up on the bus."

"You just want me to get the job so I can help pay rent."

Gianna slid her hands down, cupping Megan's ass. "You mean it? You'll move in with me?"

Megan didn't have to answer aloud. Noises started above, rhythmic thumps, suddenly interrupted by a high-pitched screaming. She pointed upward just as the thumping stopped.

"Well, let's make the most of it," Gianna said, taking Megan's hand and tugging her toward the bedroom. "And let's take our time. We have many years to come, right?"

"Yeah," Megan said, stepping behind Gianna to push her down onto the bed. "But that doesn't mean I don't want to take you fast and wet."

Gianna grabbed Megan by the upper arms and pulled her down after her, then rolled on top, straddling Megan and pinning her down onto the bed. "Slow," she whispered, planting a kiss on Megan's lips as she trailed the tips of her fingers over Megan's collarbone.

"Fast," Megan countered, plunging her hand down the front of Gianna's jeans. She was already wet and slippery, and she cried out when Megan's hands slid between her lips.

"Slow down, babe," she moaned, her fingertips gliding over Megan's breasts, her eyes drifting closed.

"Never." Megan pushed two fingers inside Gianna and pressed her thumb to her clit. "You know I'm fast and you like it."

Gianna just moaned, grinding down onto Megan's hand.

She seemed to be past the point of arguing. Megan figured she had won.

But when Gianna had finished, she took over, and she kissed every inch of Megan's body, piece by piece. Her lips were hot and wet and slow, and Megan writhed on the bed, soaked in sweat. No matter how much she begged, though, Gianna wouldn't go any faster.

As Gianna's lips closed around Megan's throbbing, swollen clit, all she could think was, *I guess I did my best.*

Share Your Thoughts

Thank you for reading Crash Into You by Diana Morland. If you enjoyed this book, please consider leaving a review on Amazon or on Goodreads. Your support means the world to our authors!

More from LoveLight Press

LoveLight Press is a small independent publisher specializing in LGBT Romance. Why not visit our website or join our mailing list to see our latest titles?

More from Diana Morland

Contemporary romance:

Beauty and the Blog

Lifetime Between Us

Paranormal romance:

In a Witch's Hands (Witches in the City, Book 1)

For a Witch's Eyes (Witches in the City, Book 2)

On a Witch's Mind (Witches in the City, Book 3)

In a Witch's Heart (Witches in the City, Book 5)

At a Witch's Back (Witches in the City, Book 4)

The Naga's Prey

Diana grew up in the beautiful, historic city of Philadelphia, and has always loved it just a little more than any other place. It was there that she discovered how great ladies are and how much fun it is to write stories that are pretty much just full of ladies. She currently resides in Maryland with her partner and their cuddly cat.

Website: http://www.dianamorland.com
Mailing List: http://eepurl.com/bwRKpz
Social Media: https://twitter.com/dianamorland
http://www.facebook.com/dianamorlandauthor
https://www.goodreads.com/user/show/46351778-diana-morland

CPSIA information can be obtained
at www.ICGtesting.com
Printed in the USA
LVHW011925260819
628959LV00015B/1440/P